Slaves of Gwaehr
Erotica & Other Curiosities

By
Eve Caldwell Black

Published in the United States of America by Kate McNamara

ISBN 978-0-578-03372-3

Printed in the United States of America by Lulu.com

Cover design by Kate McNamara

Second Edition

For my Grandmother
who kept
Steamy Books under Her Bed

Chapter 1

The war, at last, was ended. Etain stood weeping, her wrists bound firmly in front of her, and behind her lay the lost homeland of the ancient tribe of the E'Hrglaendi. From where she stood on the white sand that stretched for miles along the shore of the Bridin Sea, Etain could see the burning ruins of her father's castle, still standing high above her on the black cliffs that overlooked the ocean shore. The skyline glowed vermilion, scarlet, yellow, and black billows of smoke climbed over the Bridin plain, blowing gently out to sea.

On the sea shore Etain stood watching the evil clouds coming, the faces of the gods boiling on the breeze. A hoarse cry of sorrow rose from her breast and she could not stop it, she could not choke it down. The clouds looked like death heads in the sky. Surely she should beg to be put to the sword, rather than bear the uncertainty of the days to come.

A dry, cold wind blew. It nipped and chilled Etain through her white linen gown. Winter was coming. Upon the wind a dusting of fine snow began to swirl. The serfs had long since harvested the crops of grain and tubers, and now the vast grasslands of Bridin lay golden, dormant, as the Dark Goddess Helkara took dominion over the earth.

This had been the homeland of the E'Hrglaendi. It extended from the seashore, some fifty miles square, lying in the Basvfanian lowlands just south of the mountains of Kalohr. There it abutted the Thelkin city-state of Klaerthelke which was surrounded on all sides by a great turreted wall made from granite blocks, which were hewn from the Kalohrian mountainsides by free men. Here the terrain was steep and hilly, but to the west of the city was a fertile valley, which already lay beneath a white blanket of snow. Archers manned the wall, armed with the finest cross bows, and all traders and foreigners who would enter the city must be admitted by the guards at the great gate in the wall.

But for three hundred years the E'Hrglaendi had lived on the Bridin plain, at peace with their neighbors, farming the rich soil, with the old fortress that stood on the black cliffs their only fortification. For the last forty years Etain's father, Malkar, had been king. His rule was stern but just, and, until now, the common people had lived under the protection of his hand.

But over the last twenty years, under the leadership of Lasher the King, Gosgovnia had become great. They were an aggressive, imperialistic race, and were a formidable military power, both by land and by sea. There were five continents on the planet Gwaehr, the seventh planet from the sun in the Nu Omega Centauri star system. Gosgovnia had already conquered the free tribes and city-states on their own continent of Halkuria, and now they sent their navy and army north across the Bridin Sea to loot the riches and enslave the races of Basvfania as well. But there were factions in the Gosgovnian government that opposed this endless expansion. The people of Gosgovnia were already wealthy, and they had managed to assimilate most of the races they had subdued, making their own culture richer, in the arts and the written word. Now their cities, and the great estates of the noblemen, were renowned for their architecture and libraries and their collections of paintings and sculpture. From Thurgia they had the finest textiles, from Beuhla the finest masons on Gwaehr. The most talented scribes and poets were imported from Caehluria, and glass blowers, from the province of Trill, traveled as freemen to the Gosgovnian capital to sell their fine vases and delicate trinkets in the great market of Gelstohr.

But the factions that opposed King Lasher's imperialism were still a quiet, but persistent, voice at the royal court of Gelstohr. Elder vassals and noblemen, who had lost influence in the court when King Lasher took the throne, felt that the endless conquests of Gosgovnia were excessive, and soon the Gosgovnians would find it hard to protect their borders. Still, King Lasher had seized the might of the military, and the voices that argued for peace were over ruled, though they could not be quelled indefinitely.

And now Gosgovnia had made yet another conquest, its first on the continent of Basvfania. Etain felt tears wetting her cheeks, and with her wrists bound together, she could hardly brush them away. Although she had the wisdom of a trained priestess of Brida, her grief for her people, who had been pious and peace loving, overcame her now. Why had the Goddess allowed this to come to pass? Had their sacrifices at the temple been unpleasing? Etain remembered the joy with which she and her nineteen priestesses had celebrated each festival, and the long lines of the common folk, coming on foot or by wagon, making the little pilgrimage to the temple with their offerings of meat, produce, and wine. Surely She had found their sacrifices to be generous and fine, and She had not meted out this fate to them in anger or disdain.

Etain uttered another sob of sorrow, and the sound she made startled the soldier who was guarding her. He flinched and drew his dagger, snarling Gosgovnian obscenities. With the gleaming knife in his fist the guard spat in the sand and glared at Etain with hatred. He was tired of this war. A gnoba skin bag hung at his side. He lifted it to his mouth to drink the burning wine.

The wine was acrid and strong. As he drank it the guard stared at Etain. He found her old for a female, perhaps thirty, already far past her prime; yet he knew why she had been spared as he looked at her. For she was beautiful still, willowy and tall, with skin like cream and the most remarkable hair, all fiery copper waves that wafted over her pale arms, hiding her face as she wept.

A fine prize, he had to admit it. She was a chieftain's daughter, a healer and a sooth-sayer. He had heard tales of the priestess Etain, and of her two sisters. It was said these three beauties, all with flaming hair and skin like snow, served the Great Goddess of the E'Hrglaendi. The other two were younger. He wondered what had become of them as he stared at Etain.

But it humiliated him to be left to watch her, and besides this, he was superstitious about lingering after the battle was won. He wouldn't feel easy until they boarded the ship with the few wretched prisoners they had taken, and so he soothed himself with the wine in the gnoba skin bag. The wine made him bolder until he wouldn't look away from the red-haired woman, this prize that was meant for Lasher, king of all Gosgovnia.

It was true, he knew, that no child had ever opened her womb, that her secret places had never been penetrated by a man. King Lasher would surely keep this one for himself, rather than give her off as reward to some vassal or other.

He wondered when Lasher would open her. Perhaps he would deflower her at the festival of Baeul some weeks hence. Or yet again, thought the soldier, the king might take the woman into his cabin immediately. The king's cabin was fitted with a place where a prisoner could be properly restrained, and the opening of a slave made for pleasurable diversion after such an arduous campaign.

Through the light snowfall Etain could see the yellow glaze of the sun as it set behind the clouds. Before her the Gosgovnian longboats were beached, waiting to be filled with the miserable prisoners the Gosgovnians had taken, a handful of her father's serfs and a few women and children, all crying piteously for their lives. The longboats would take them to the Gosgovnian war ship which lay anchored beyond the surf, upon the silver water of the sea.

Among the soldiers, who were now occupied with guarding the prisoners, Etain saw one man who stood a head taller than nearly all the men. He was wearing a heavy cloak of purple wool over his Gosgovnian breastplate of leather and brass. His thick black hair and beard were grizzled with silver, and Etain thought his smile cruel as he surveyed his captives. His cloak was held in place across his shoulders with a silver fibula laid with rubies, worked into the likeness of the head of a beast, but Etain could not tell from where she stood what beast it might be. He called out orders to the other men, and Etain could see from his manner and bearing that he must be Lasher, the Gosgovnian king.

Now the guards began to herd them towards the longboats, and a fresh wave of sorrow washed over her heart; for all the people she had known, nearly every one, were dead. Never again would she see their fair faces as she presided over the rites of the holy days, never again would she tend them in their sickness and their pain. The temple of the Great Triple Goddess Brida, with its megaliths of black granite and its arches of lapis lazuli, had been desecrated and made vile. Even if her rightful station were restored to her Etain did not know how she could ever make it holy again.

A wave of crying and wailing broke out as the hostages were forced into the longboats. Etain longed to comfort her people, but the guards kept her from them, as if knowing with certainty that her presence among them would encourage them even in slavery. The longboats were filled, and then the last of the fleet gnobas that Lasher's soldiers had ridden to victory were led into the surf, to be brought through the waves to the side of the Gosgovnian ship where they could be harnessed and hoisted back on board.

Etain was put into the very last longboat with seven hardened soldiers to guard her. In the very first longboat Etain could see the king standing, his silhouette angular and tall as the light of the setting sun began to fade.

Etain calmed herself and prepared to meet her fate. Her gentle and wise heart knew that all forms were mutable, and that the fortunes of men might ever change. As the longboats approached the warrior ship she thought of the dead, and wished them good passage to the place where the mist meets the sea.

But her sisters, Thildin and Olara, were not dead; of this she was sure. Although they were separated in age by several years, they were as close as if they had shared the womb at the same time. Also they looked remarkably alike. Etain, who was the eldest, had trained and tutored Thildin and Olara in the ways of the learned priestesses of Brida. Thildin, who was the second eldest, was more like Etain, independent and thoughtful, though Thildin had a fiery temper and was prone to anger easily. But Olara was still very young, impressionable, and immature. Etain worried that she might not fare well on her own, separated from loved ones and friends. Still, Etain felt certain that somehow they would be safe from danger. They would be separated for a long time, but she felt with the Sight that they lived, and would one day meet again.

They reached the side of the great Gosgovnian ship. Its prow was decorated with the head of a snarling wolf. This was fearsome to see, the eyes painted with pupils of blood red, the jaws drawn back to show the fangs glistening gray. It was, no doubt, the image of some magical animal, or perhaps the head of some Gosgovnian war god, unknown to the people of Etain.

She felt the large hands of the drunken guard upon her and again she was tied, first with a rope around her knees and then with another at her ankles as well. The rough hemp bit into her flesh where it lay against her bare skin and burned through the flimsy fabric of her gown. Then the soldier tied her arms, with a rope that passed over her elbows, so that they were bound down tightly against her body.

She was helpless then, but the soldier wasn't satisfied. Another rope was passed around the small of her back so that her wrists, which were tied together still, lay firmly against the softest part of her thighs. Then yet another rope to bind her arms, and this one passed sharply beneath her breasts so that the nipples stood up and showed themselves through her dress; and Etain felt a hot flush of color rising to her cheeks.

As the soldier handled Etain he felt a fullness in his cock so that he was very conscious of it pricking up against his trousers. For a moment he let his fingers close hard around the small pale arms, and he thought of Etain tied the way he would so much like to tie her, but he dared not fondle her, for he knew Etain was to be saved for the king.

Etain and the rest of the hostages were driven into the hull of the ship, but there was a special dark place where Etain was forced to lie alone, and for three days she lay in the filthy straw, her hands and feet firmly bound. Sometimes an old woman brought her cold porridge and water, but Etain was ill with the motion of the ship, and was unable to eat. After a long while the nausea began to pass. Etain slept fitfully then, her dream world peopled by the dead, and by the grinning, hideous faces of the Underworld Goddess Thrice Three, who had brought her to this low place to lie.

On the third night the old woman unbound her ankles and led her out of the lowest levels of the ship, and Etain found herself in a room all made of cedar wood with draperies of burgundy and gold brocade, and a great mahogany bed all hung with Thurgic silk. The air here was fresh, smelling sweetly of the cedar wood. Etain breathed deeply of it to make the feeling of sickness pass from her body. There was a small window through which poured the healing rays of the afternoon sun, and Etain went and stood in this pyramid of light, until the sickly trembling began to leave her limbs, and the crawling died away from her skin.

This was the cabin of King Lasher, of this Etain was sure. It was furnished all in mahogany, each piece worked intricately and polished to a soft dark glow. Etain saw that the legs of the table and chairs were carved into the likeness of the feet of wolves as were the legs of the bed. On the walls there hung four heavy tapestries, a coat-of-arms bearing the image of a running wolf pierced through with a golden staff; and though the blood flowed from his heart Etain saw in all the tapestries that the wolf was immortal still, the magical beast that housed the soul of the warrior-king.

Now Etain felt certain that she had been spared to become the concubine of the king. Her heart filled with loathing and doubt as she thought of his cruel face smiling over his captives. She looked at the tapestries of the wolf pierced through with the staff, and suddenly she thought of the silver fibula the king wore on his cloak. Surely it must be worked as the likeness of a wolf as well, for all around her, and even at the prow of the ship, this was the most striking emblem honored by Gosgovnia. This symbol of violence filled her with revulsion, but she fought to calm herself, for she was sure that now she had been called to serve dark Helkara the Crone, and only through acceptance could she ever master her destiny.

There was a small wooden tub by the fireplace and to this the old woman led Etain. There the old woman undressed her and gestured for her to sit down inside; and so Etain was washed, her long hair and her smooth skin, with perfumed soaps and clear water scented with the petals of flowers.

The hot water was good, and though she would not untie her hands, the old woman held a goblet of sweet-smelling wine for Etain to drink from. Etain swallowed eagerly and soon she felt its effects in her body, a spreading warmth and a softening of her sore limbs; and when her bath was finished, Etain was given a clean shift and a chair by the glow of the fire, and the old woman fed her a savory fish pie.

Then she was made to lie down upon the bed, and the old woman tied the end of the rope that bound her hands to a brass ring that was fitted into the wall. The old woman left her there and Etain was alone. The room was filled with shadows now, the bright orange hues of the cedar wood deepening to blood red; and Etain felt a core of fear growing in the pit of her heart as she lay in the great bed in the darkening room, awaiting the return of the king.

For some hours Etain slept; but she awoke to find the old woman stirring the coals of the fire until the flames leapt up white and brilliant in the blackness. Etain became aware of the lapping of the waves against the hull of the ship, of the gentle rocking of the ship upon the waves. The old woman lit the tallow candles, one by one, that stood in many brackets on the walls of the cedar wood room.

The room glowed red-gold in the candlelight. The old woman opened the mahogany wardrobe, and from where she lay on the bed, Etain could see that it was full of female garments, lengths of gossamer glinting with threads of gold and silver, and bejeweled halters to bind the breasts of a woman; and she imagined that she would be dressed in these garments in preparation for the coming of the king.

And Etain saw something else inside the wardrobe, a curious device of carved wood and upholstery; yet another invention of Gosgovnia, the likes of which Etain had never seen.

It was higher than a bed, and smaller as well, yet it didn't seem to be a proper chair. When it was pulled away from the back of the wardrobe it rested on a pedestal of carved wolves' feet, and there were arm rests on both sides. These were fitted with heavy leather straps with great buckles, as were two vertical bars that extended from the lower edge of the richly upholstered cushion.

Etain stood in front of the mirror as the old woman dressed her. There was a dusting of scented powder for the puff of hair on her sex, and a binder of whalebone for her breasts, with nary enough fabric to hide the dark pink nipples. The old woman fastened her tightly into this so that the white mounds popped up like ripe pears. Her hair was brushed out and her lips and nipples were rouged.

Then came the skirt of sheer silk that hung from a circlet of tassels at her hips, glistening over her white thighs, over the red secret hair with the dark red sex inside. The skirt was made of panels, two in front and two behind, so that it parted on each side to bare her legs; or, to bare her sex, it could be parted from the front or from behind.

Etain saw herself in the glass and she was beautiful indeed; and in her own eyes she saw the dark light of the Shaeul-n'a-Gog shining. Though a part of her was filled with dread, it was her fate, and she must put herself into the hands of the Crone Goddess Helkara.

She was led to the wall, and the old woman tied her ankles, and then her wrists were tied to a brass ring over her head; and so she awaited the coming of the king.

How long Etain waited she could not tell. She was weary, but she kept herself straight and tall, murmuring incantations to the copulating Helkara. The chamber door opened and the king entered the room. To Etain's surprise, he spoke to her in broken E'Hrglaendi, which in all these days Etain hadn't heard anymore.

Lasher looked at the red-haired woman with the hunger of an animal.

He detected the fine trembling in her limbs, how her breath quickened as he approached her; and yet this one tried to hide her apprehension. It excited him to see her pushed up breasts with the erect, rouged nipples, and beneath his tunic he felt his pleasure and his desire growing.

While she was still tied Lasher took her nipples between his fingertips. Gently he pressed, until she gave a little moan and her lips parted. He wanted her legs to part also, but her ankles were tied; yet the nipples were good, and now he must have his tongue in her mouth as well.

He pushed her against the wall, her body small and soft beneath him. His fingers parted the silken skirt behind her. He cupped her satin bottom in the palms of his two hands and lifted her towards him, pressing her firmly against the cock that was hard and eager to open her.

And now he must wet her sex. He untied her hands and carried her to the bed, and Etain uttered not a sound as he cradled her. Again she was tied to the ring of brass, and her feet to the bedposts as well. The panels of the skirt were lifted away, and Lasher put a pillow beneath her knees so that her sex would be easily available to him.

Lasher undressed himself, and Etain was sure that now the opening would come; but Lasher laid himself down by her side and kissed her, long slow thrusts of his tongue. With his big hands he stroked her belly and fingered her puff of red hair, until Etain felt her secret cunt-place plumping, softening, to yield to the poking Lasher would give her. His fingers then, tender, parting the wet folds of delicate flesh, darting in and stretching, probing, exploring, preparing the way for the maidenhead to be broken, almost without pain.

But it was time for Etain to see the cock that would open her. Lasher straddled her throat so that the big cock bobbed against her chin. Then he slid his cock forward so that the tip was pressed against her soft white cheek; and Etain trembled as she kissed the throbbing shaft, her mouth admitting the tip of Lasher's prick. Timidly she licked the dull cock head of the king, smelling the delicate musky odor of his seed, and tasting the salty droplet of semen on her tongue.

The king thought he must surely take her now, and yet a chieftain's daughter must be opened in the ritual way. Though the public deflowering would not take place for weeks, yet the maidenhead must be ruptured on the opening table. Naked, he stood up from the bed and untied her, leading her trembling form to the device.

But before he tied her down, he took her face in his hands, and Etain saw that beneath his dark brow his eyes were the most remarkable brilliant blue. He kissed her again, deeply and slowly, so that her limbs were too soft to resist him, and then he pushed her belly down onto the brocade cushion, fastening her wirsts and elbows on either side. Eagerly he spread her thighs, to be strapped to the wooden bars below.

And now Lasher would bare the snow-white bottom and see the wet sex of Etain. For this he lifted the silken panels of the delicate skirt away. He spoke softly to her and slid a long finger inside.

Her whole sex could be seen very well now, shell-pink and glistening, and when he pressed with his finger he could see the hole, which excited him; but before he penetrated with his cock he used his thumb, dipping it into the cunt-folds to moisten it well. His thumb would be needed to open the other nether hole, which must also be thoroughly probed.

Lasher guided the head of his cock to rest against the exposed sex of Etain, and gently he rocked his hips so that the cock head pushed softly on the maidenhead. At the same time he used his thumb to open the brown hole, and Etain moaned with pleasure, for she had never known the bliss of Helkara until now.

Then there came the moment when King Lasher felt the brown hole open completely, and Etain's body was limp upon the device. This was the moment for the opening, the time for the maidenhead to give way at last; and so the cock head plunged in, and Etain uttered a sharp, short cry.

But then Lasher's arms were around her neck and his hands caressed her face and hair. In soft, low tones he spoke to her and comforted her, pumping her tenderly with his cock, treating the ruined maidenhead with care.

Etain felt her body grow soft again, and Lasher fingered her all the while, but presently his words became moans. Powerfully he thrusted now, pulling her hips against him, burying his prick in her sex, until finally he gave her his seed and was satisfied.

And so Etain was deflowered. Lasher released her from the device and undressed her. Tenderly he kissed her and smoothed her hair. Surely he does not think of himself as cruel, thought Etain, for he takes great care to pleasure his women, even though she be but a slave.

The king slept then, but Etain lay awake and felt the rocking of the ship on the waves. Now she was one with Helkara, the Dark Mother, and her destiny lay in a country far off across the sea. Perhaps if she pleased the king her life as a slave would not be too miserable. She thought again of her sisters Olara and Thildin, and with anxiety she wondered what their fate at the hands of the Gosgovnians had been. Surely, surely they must still be alive. But how would she reach them, how would she find them again? Would her captors allow her to practice the arts by which she prophesied through the Seeing Eye? She lay awake in the dark, uncertain, until fatigue finally blessed her with deep, dreamless sleep; and the great war ship with the head of the wolf at its prow sailed on through the moonless night, bringing her ever closer to the fate of a slave of Gosgovnia.

Chapter 2

In the mountain city of Klaerthelke every soul was preparing for the festival of Baeul. They gathered purple glorni flowers, so plentiful on the Kalohrian hillsides, and garnished each windowsill in the city with the pungent, fragrant petals. In the steep, narrow streets bleached white linens hung from the second story windows of old houses to dry in the fresh spring breeze. To the east and north the craggy granite peaks of the Kalohrian Mountains towered blue gray in the sunshine, still capped with a blanket of white snow. To the south the vast expanse of the Bridin plain was green again as the grasses and wildflowers began to sprout from the soggy dark soil, thawing now in the warmth of the sun. Thelkin children, dressed in traditional hooded shirts embroidered with brightly colored thread, played hide-and-catch-can in the garbage littered alleyways behind the rows of stone dwellings that rose two or three stories tall. From every winding street came the sounds of footfalls and laughter echoing from the high buildings in the thin mountain air. In the town square jugglers and musicians applied their trades, all for a few copper coins tossed into small, polished chests lined with velvet of burgundy or blue. The street corners were coming alive as the snow melted on the dirty cobblestones with crude wooden carts drawn by gentle gnobas. The beasts wore red leather harnesses festooned with tassels of blue and green and gold. Fish and sausage from Oslopa, and all imaginable dried fruits and meats, were sold from these homemade carts. The merchants shouted and called for everyone to come buy, everyone to leave the dark, musty houses of stone and thatch, and bathe their faces in the sunshine of the new spring. At the city gate the traffic of merchants, traders, and foreigners had begun, and outside the gate of the city, at the base of the sloping road that led into town, the white alien ships could be seen where they were stationed, all gleaming rhenium diboride and chrome. In the valley the deep snow had melted, and the delicate green fuzz of new spring grass could be seen. It had been three moons since the taking of E'Hrglaend.

Olara stood in an alleyway, peering around the walls of an ancient Thelkin dwelling. All winter long Olara had lived on the streets of Klaerthelke like one of the orphans who ran in packs everywhere in the city. She was glad in the thin warmth of the spring day, glad for surviving the carnage that had all but exterminated her people. It was a feeling she had not felt in many weeks, not even in the smallest measure. She had found it hard to be alone with only the company of bedraggled beggars to give her solace. Except for her newly begun training in the convent of Brida this harsh winter had been her first taste of life outside her father's castle. Now that the winter was over she was overcoming some of her fears and grief, and she found herself relishing this bit of freedom, a feeling she had never known under the guidance of her elders.

The bright sunlight also infused her wildest schemes. From where she stood, high on the hilly street between the tall houses, she could see the towers of the alien ships on the horizon, the spires visible beyond the city wall. She thought of her two sisters and felt sure they must be captives of the Gosgovnian army. Only she, the youngest and least experienced, had been destined to remain free. She could not scry, like Etain, and she had learned only the most basic of magic spells, not nearly enough to affect the outcome of such a serious situation. How ironic this life can be, she thought, that the most fearful challenges should be left in the hands of novices. She looked again at the spires of the alien ships. Somehow she would get permission to approach them.

But the day was glorious, and her stomach was burbling with hunger. She turned her attention to the nearest cart of food. Its merchant was young and tall. Although she could only see him from behind she could see that beneath his undyed homespun shirt his shoulders were broad and his waist was narrow. His cart was hung with big sausages and garlic. Olara began to feel yet another new sensation as she looked at the food and the young man.

She thought she would creep up and have a look. He had a beautiful head of dark brown curly hair. She looked down at herself, and saw her round breasts covered in dirty sackcloth. Self-consciously she smoothed back the fiery locks of her hair, wondering if she, a novitiate of Brida, was still presentable to a man. In the old days, she thought, we would have turned him away from our circle without a second look; but now it was if she saw through new eyes, and, freed from the fetters of tradition and authority, her mind and body began to respond in a wholly different way.

She had still not ventured from the alley, but she imagined herself standing next to him. She found herself imagining slipping her slender white fingers underneath the young man's homespun shirt, and she could almost feel her cool palms against his warm, soft skin. She could feel him shiver as she ran her fingers along his sides to his nipples, and she thought he would flinch as she pinched them, brick brown and firm like pebbles. He would hold his breath as she ran her hands back down again, down into the black curly hair, fingering and rubbing between his legs. The big cock would bob and jump as she tried to grasp it with her hands, and then her tongue would lick the tip, tasting the first salty pearl of his manhood.

She imagined this as she stood there in the bright spring day, and she felt a warm, moist spot forming inside her sex. In the convent she knew that the fully-fledged priestesses were trained in the arts of fertility as well as magic, but she had never expected to have such feelings outside that context. In a few days all the world would celebrate Baeul, the festival of the great virgin goddess Brida, and bonfires would burn and couples would walk towards each other and be wed; but Olara found herself thinking of Ultaine, when men and women, mad with desire, paired randomly in the dark. She was free now, no convent held her. Perhaps this young man could be hers. She imagined he had a handsome face, with large, black eyes and a full, sensuous mouth. Perhaps they, like the others, would wander into the dark green woods and lay together, in honor of the Mother Goddess Kerridorah and her horned consort, Kernulos.

Again she smoothed her hair. She must approach him; she must see the face framed beneath the dark locks of hair. Cautiously she came out of the alleyway, and slowly she walked toward the cart and the unknown prince. She made a large circle around him, and finally she came into his view and met him face to face.

Her eyes fell upon his face, and suddenly Olara's feet were rooted to the ground. She felt herself transported to another place as much as if the aliens were to take her away in a ship. Surely there had never been such a face, never in all the lands of Basvfania.

His eyes were large and luminous, and ultimately a little sad, but instead of being black or brown, they were deep blue, fringed with thick black lashes. He was fair of skin, with a straight, aquiline nose and high cheekbones. His mouth was full and sensuous as she had imagined. It curved into a soft smile when he saw her. She was so conscious of her bedraggled appearance that she didn't know what to say.

"Hello," she said, unable to take her eyes away from his face.

She could feel him looking her over, but she saw no judgment in his expression, either of approval or dissatisfaction. As he looked at her she felt her confidence growing.

"Hello," he said.

Now that Olara stood in front of the cart she could see that he sold more than sausage. There was also smoked fish and jerky as well as fragrant meat pies. Olara had not eaten a proper meal since she had escaped the last battle on the Bridin plain. She had managed to beg a few copper coins from the richer citizens of Klaerthelke, and these she kept in a leather pouch tied around her slim waist with a thong. Hungrily she sniffed the meat pies.

"How much?" she said.

The young man looked at Olara, admiring the beauty he saw beneath the dirty rags she wore. Although life had given her a lowly condition this gorgeous creature stood straight and tall and proud. He saw that she was about to reach into her small leather bag. Surely it could hold but a few copper pennies, for he guessed she was a beggar. He would have given her a gift of food, but he thought this might hurt her pride. Perhaps, after she had eaten, he could get her to tell him her name. He decided to adjust the price of his fine meat pies to what he thought she could afford. How much was too little, and therefore a mockery to this angel in beggar's garb? He hoped the little bag held two copper coins.

"Two pennies, Miss," he said, and as he saw the smile of gladness which Olara smiled he felt a lightness come upon him, and happily he let Olara choose a pie. Immediately she took it and devoured it hungrily.

"My name is Gol," he said, as Olara ate her pie, which was hardly a meal for one who must be half starved. "Perhaps," he said, "you would be so kind as to try some of this sausage. It is not Oslopan, and I haven't sold any yet. It is homemade. My mother and I keep a few menka on our small farm."

While Olara ate she listened, enraptured by his baritone voice. She was incredulous at her good fortune. She nodded and he pulled down a brown sausage and cut it for her. He had told her his name! She ate the delicious food and gazed upon the beautiful young man. Surely the gods were with her. She had lived to see this bright spring day.

She was inclined to lick her fingers, but this did not befit a woman of her natural station.

"My name is Olara," she said, while she still held a bit of sausage in her hand. "The sausage is delicious. It is easily just as good as any I have ever had from Oslopa."

This last, of course, was something of a small fib since Olara had never had Oslopan sausage. The E'Hrglaendi had never been fond of trade. But Olara was fond of smoked menka flesh, although they made foul farm animals. Her father, Malkar, had let his serfs hunt them for him, for they raised an impenetrable stench when domesticated. She had always wondered about this, that the Thelkins kept them in pens, but then she knew that menka were ferocious and dangerous in the wild.

She felt so good now that he had told him her name. Her copper hair shone in the sun. Gol aroused her sensuality in a way that she knew belonged exclusively to the goddess Helkara. Suddenly she wanted to tell him everything.

"Where are you from?" asked Gol. He thought she must be a newly made gypsy, for he had never seen her in the city square before.

"Gosgovnia has taken my people," she said.

For a moment Gol did not reply. Could she be speaking of the conquered kingdom of E'Hrglaend?

"Surely you can't be E'Hrglaendi," he said. "We heard that the few survivors of the last battle were taken as prisoners of war."

"No, not all," she said. "There were a few of us who were not within the castle walls when it was over run by the Gosgovnians. I was with a sister of Brida tending the sick wife of a serf on my father's land. When we saw the smoke rising from the castle the peasants put us into a cart and covered us with skins and brought us here. The nun who was my teacher died of the brain fever so I am alone. And my father, and my two sisters … I don't know what has become of them."

Gol was amazed. Here was the daughter of a once mighty chieftain. Immediately he wanted to give her aide, but at the same time he had a vague, nagging fear that perhaps this might provoke a reprisal from the Gosgovnians upon his people.

"Have you spoken of this to anyone?" he said.

"No, I haven't."

"Let's keep it so. You must come with me and be my guest," he said. He thought what an honor it would be for himself and his old, blind mother, to shelter this creature of nobility and beauty.

Olara tarried by the cart until sunset. Gol was gracious and kind to all the people who came to shop. Even one of the aliens came to buy from Gol. He came with a companion, and Olara was excited as she watched him approach the cart in his shiny black uniform. She had never seen an alien, but Gol knew him by name. The aliens wore small, shiny weapons at their sides. Olara eyed these with awe. It seemed absurd that these weapons could be more powerful than the swords and arrows of the Gosgovnian army, but even in the land of the E'Hrglaendi she had heard this was so.

At sunset nearly all the goods were sold, and Gol motioned for her to climb into the front seat of the wagon beside him. They sat together, shoulder to shoulder and never said a word; but Gol was thinking of Olara's virgin body, and imagined himself pulling away the ragged sackcloth shift she wore to expose two perfect round breasts and a firm, white belly.

Gol drove the gnoba up a rough trail upon the green mountainside. The cart shook and rattled as the wooden wheels went over stones in the path. Between the wheel ruts grew new green grass, and along the side of the road bunches of white and purple wild flowers had already sprung from the warm soil. They traveled on for a mile or so, and then Olara saw the farmhouse made of stone, thatched with a thick roof of rushes.

There was a chimney, and a thin ribbon of smoke trailed out upon the breeze. The gnoba stopped in front of a watering trough and a pump, and Gol got out of the cart and pumped some water for the beast to drink. Olara could not wait to go inside where she imagined the room would be cozy and warm.

It was warm inside and dark. There was a table and four chairs, a bed, and a wooden ladder that led into a loft. Beside the fire there was an old woman sitting in a rocker.

"Gol?" the old woman said, as the door opened and they stepped inside.

"Yes, Mother," said Gol. "I've brought a guest. She can help us with the cooking and housekeeping."

The woman stood up from her rocker.

"Who is she?" the old woman said. She did not look at them, but only faced them, and Olara saw that she was blind.

"This is Olara," said Gol, "and she has to stay with us, for she's the daughter of Malkar, the E'Hrglaendi chieftain. She has no where else to go."

"Malkar?" the old woman gasped. For a moment Olara felt unsure. What if this old matriarch did not want her to stay? But she looked at Gol, and her eyes met his, and she knew he would not let her go.

"It's all right," he said. "No one else will know who she is. She can earn her keep helping with the chores."

The old woman smiled.

"Welcome, Olara," she said, "My name is Glendin."

Olara was glad then, for now she could see the possibility of a new life. She wanted to go to the fireside and embrace Glendin, but she did not, thinking that it might be improper; but she was sure that soon she would greet this woman as mother-in-law.

After supper, Olara lay in the bed in the loft. She waited in anticipation for the sound of Gol opening the door. Surely he would come to her tonight. She remembered the way his blue eyes had caressed her in her shift that day. She knew he wanted her naked, two round breast mounds before him, the nipples erect and ready for licking. He wanted her naked in front of him, with her long, white legs tucked under her firm, round behind, the coppery nether hairs peeping out upon her flat young belly.

Finally she heard the creaking of the door, and Gol appeared with a lamp in his hand. He padded softly past his sleeping mother and called for Olara in a hushed voice. Full of happiness Olara sprang from the bed and leaned over the edge of the loft. When she saw his face she was so full of gladness she could hardly contain herself.

"Take the lamp," he whispered.

Olara took the lamp, and Gol climbed up the ladder, and then he took her to the bedside, and they sat down.

"My love!" he said, and then he kissed her, a deep, probing kiss, thrusting his tongue into her mouth, quieting a dark voice in Olara that she had never heard before.

Then his hands were on her breasts, pressing and rubbing, pushing her down onto the bed of rushes in the loft. She felt him slip his strong hands inside her shift, and then she felt him run his fingers from her navel to her nipples. She shivered and parted her legs ever so slightly. He pressed her down and down, and then she felt the delicious sensation of his entire weight upon her slender body. He pinned her, and then he kissed her deeply. He took her small wrists in his big hands and stretched her arms over her head and secured them there.

"I thought you would never come," said Olara.

"I had to be with you," said Gol.

He let go of her wrists and worked his fingers down into the warm coppery hair. Very gently he parted the lips of her love blossom, and tenderly he inserted one long, slender finger. Slowly and carefully he pumped, caressing the wet cunt folds behind the maidenhead. Olara pulled his face to hers and kissed him. Their tongues entwined like two young vines seeking the sunlight. With her hand she felt his big cock inside his trousers bumping and hopping against her belly. She wanted him to take her, but instead he let her go and sat up on the bed.

"You will be mine," he said. "We will be hand fasted on Baeul, and you will be my wife, and until that day I'll burn for you day and night."

"And I for you," Olara said softly.

"We'll seek out a private place in the woods away from the bonfires, and I will have your maidenhead, and our love will be a benediction to the Great Goddess Brida."

And now Olara knew that she was truly blessed. She was amazed at this wonderful man who would curb his desire to serve the Goddess. Her life in the convent of Brida was far away and forever in her past.

Then Gol pulled her towards him, and kissed her and caressed her, before he took the lamp to return to his bed in the stable.

"I won't come to you every night," he said, "but don't worry. It's only that I couldn't contain my desire for you if I were to be near you like this night after night. I would take you and open you before the appointed time, and rob our union of the blessing of the new year."

"I'll gladly wait until you are my lawful husband," said Olara, " and every day I'll think of the union of our bodies until the day finally comes that I can be yours."

And with that Gol kissed her again. Then quietly he left her; but it was some time before Olara fell asleep, feeling warm and well fed in the little stone farmhouse on the green mountainside.

Chapter 3

It was daybreak. In the queen's palace, Thildin knelt before the altar of Sillessa, the little virgin goddess of the Gosgovnians. The altar was fine, gilded and bejeweled, and draped with blue and green silks from the captured city-state of Thurgia. It stood beneath a window that over looked the royal garden, catching the first rays of the morning sun. It was fitted with a wrought-iron candelabra that held twenty votive candles, kept burning by the women of the harem when they came to the altar to pray. On the center of the table was a place for other offerings as well, wine or fruit, made by petitioners who had special favors to ask of the goddess. It was small in scale, but grand in design. This was a fitting place to worship for the daughters and wives of King Lasher.

Thildin brought her offering of red wine. Her large breasts were bound in green velvet and gold silk. Over the top of the lacey brassiere the round nipples peeped out like gumdrops. Her waist was draped with layers of filmy golden cloth that exposed her long, white legs, but hid the fiery bright cushion of hair between them. This was an immodest costume for a nun of Brida; yet Thildin knew she would always serve the Goddess, as Virgin or as Crone, however She demanded.

In the first days of her enslavement Thildin had found life in captivity very hard. In the queen's palace she was kept well fed and warm, and she hadn't been forced to do labor, because she was the daughter of a king; but still, her fiercely independent spirit rebelled against her confinement in the harem. I should be preparing to observe the rites of Baeul, she thought, instead of sitting here within these four walls dressed in these doll's clothes at the command of men. Every day since her capture she had forced herself to choke down her anger. Afraid of provoking a cruel reprisal she had, for many weeks, tried to keep to herself, and she talked very little to the other women of the harem except when directly spoken to. Two of the king's young wives, Halla and Vanda, in particular, had tried to comfort to her in this strange land; but Thildin could not accept their affection, thinking they only felt sorry for her. At least, she thought, I have not had to endure the sexual advances of a man; for, unlike Etain, who had welcomed the petitions of all her people, Thildin had solely preferred the company of women. And so she forced herself to be calm, to be patient, while the hours and days passed tediously by; but within her, her heart raged to be free.

The two royal palaces, with the gorgeous garden that lay between them, stood on a hilltop overlooking the Gosgovnian capital of Gelstohr. The garden was exquisite, with carefully manicured lawns and many beds of exotic flowers. In the center of the garden was a magnificent fountain, sculpted of pink marble with the likeness of a young girl catching flowing water in her cupped hands. Four walkways paved with sparkling sand stone led away from the fountain in the cardinal directions, north, east, south, and west. These crossed the immense expanse of lawn, perhaps a thousand feet. Beside the walkways were the flowerbeds which the gardeners had already planted with colorful plants grown from seedlings during the cooler months in the royal hot house. There were red and white hearts-o'-flame, and delicate babies' tears of lavender and blue. In the summer months there would be orange and yellow shaerl lilies, and pettifore blossoms of red violet and pale pink. Green and blue hassa grass grew around the base of the fountain with its tendrils of tiny white and pink flowers swaying gracefully in the breeze. There were goba plants too, spreading thickly upon the soil, creating a rich carpet of shiny purple blossoms where the walkways met the borders of the flowerbeds.

The king's palace stood on the east side of the garden. It was built of creamy Beuhlan stone, imported from that province, which lay some seventy miles west of Gelstohr. King Lasher had commissioned it as soon as he took the throne, and many ancient buildings had been plundered for items to ornament this luxurious dwelling. It was a rectangular building, with a central portico of arches, rising three stories tall and extending the entire length of the garden lawns. Above the portico were two rows of seven arched windows. The rest of the palace's three hundred rooms occupied the two long wings that jutted out from the portico, north and south, on either side of the main wing. There were five large banquet halls where the king was wont to entertain, furnished with long mahogany tables, richly upholstered chairs, and plush sofas where guests could recline between courses. For every festival and political gathering the celebrations were lavish and costly. The Gosgovnians were fond of rich food and strong drink. The palace also housed the ambassadors from all the provinces of Halkuria, as well as scribes, accountants, runners, chefs, and slaves. Behind the king's palace, but still within the great wall that encompassed the royal complex, lay the stables, where Gosgovnian gnobas, large and fleet, were fed and tended. The Gosgovnian army owed much of its success to these well-bred animals. In fact their cavalry had no match upon the planet of Gwaehr.

The queen's palace stood on the west side of the garden and was similar in design to the king's palace although somewhat smaller. It was designed to completely isolate the king's women from all males. Here the wives, daughters, concubines, and slaves of King Lasher lived in various degrees of luxury. Most of King Lasher's seventy-three wives had their own chambers, although not all of them had their own sitting rooms. King Lasher had seven daughters, and each of them occupied their own suite of three rooms, including a sleeping chamber, a sitting room, and a bath. Lasher's concubines and slaves shared four large chambers, sleeping together on mats on the floor, and they were confined and were not given the run of the palace. Thildin was kept in the last and largest dormitory on the northern end of the palace and found herself restricted to only three rooms.

But on this morn Thildin had risen early while the other women still slept. She had a special task to perform that must be done in secret. After she had made her offering of wine she placed a large crystal bowl filled with clear water upon the altar. Her heart pounded as she gazed into the bowl, fearing she might be caught. The water was dark in the half-light, and for a long time she stared into the water, trying to see what had become of her two sisters. It was a technique she had sometimes used with success in the temple of Brida, but now it yielded her nothing. Scrying had been Etain's strong suit, with her gift for prophecy, while Thildin had always been best at magic. Olara was merely a child, not even out of her teens, and had only begun her training when their father's kingdom fell. In the confinement of King Lasher's harem, Thildin had nothing to work with. Her knowledge of medicine and magic was all for naught. Still she was certain her sisters still lived. She only hoped that somehow they could reach each other again.

With a sigh Thildin gave up her scrying. She was not a woman who accepted failure easily, and momentarily she felt herself overwhelmed by frustration that she could not complete her task. She removed the scrying bowl from the altar and stored it again with the other objects sacred to Sillessa. She could still feel her heart beating, and now she realized she was trembling as well. I will not allow myself to have these feelings of self-doubt, she thought. I must be strong, today of all days. For my audience with Princess Riedl. I will calm myself with prayer.

Thildin knelt before the altar and collected her thoughts. The statuette of Sillessa was beautiful indeed, painted and clothed in white and silver silk. Thildin's people knew her as the virgin aspect of the Triple Goddess Brida, but Sillessa was far less powerful, since the Gosgovnians gave supremacy to the gods. Thildin bowed her head in reverence to Brida, the Goddess she knew.

I pray to you, as the Goddess of War, to free my people.

I pray to you, as the Goddess of Healing, to attend and comfort the wounded.

I pray to you, as the Goddess of Smith Craft, to help my people rebuild a nation.

With this prayer, Thildin calmed herself in preparation for her audience with Princess Riedl, the youngest daughter of Lasher the King. Thildin could only guess what the princess had in mind for her. Through the window above the shrine Thildin could still see the three moons of Gweahr, each one making its descent in the sky.

As she was kneeling before the altar, two slaves came to attend her. They motioned for her to rise, and then she was led through a draped doorway leading to parts of the palace where Thildin had never been before. The slaves led her down a long corridor paneled with gleaming mahogany. Through arched windows Thildin saw the rays of the new morning sun. They passed tapestry after tapestry, and each one was magnificent. Some depicted warriors engaged in battle, while others rendered gardens of rare flowers and extraordinary birds. They passed likenesses of queens and princesses enthroned on purple cushions and attended by many slaves; but the most powerful image of all was the icon of the war god Balkohr, the running wolf whose side was pierced by a golden staff.

The slaves brought Thildin to a chamber. Windowless, it was brightly lit with tapers held by brass sconces on the wall. As Thildin entered the room she first saw a great bed with a high mahogany headboard that was carved into the familiar likeness of the head of the snarling wolf. The bed frame was mahogany as well, with four tall bedposts, carved into artful spindles that rose gracefully upward. A silken coverlet of black and gold covered the mattresses of eiderdown. The bed stood against the western wall of the chamber so it was centered in the room, and at each side there stood a gorgeous table. There was another table as well, taller and longer than the tables by the bed, and at each end of this there stood a chair upholstered in black silk and worked with delicate embroidery of gold thread. Between the sconces of candles Thildin saw that iron rings had been mounted on the walls. Everywhere that Thildin looked she saw the likeness of Balkohr, for the legs of the great bed and tables were carved like the paws of the wolf. Thildin guessed this was a private chamber of the Princess Riedl, a place where Riedl could please herself without influencing the rest of the harem. Thildin knew that Princess Riedl was King Lasher's favorite daughter, and that he indulged her every wish.

The slaves tied Thildin's wrists together, lashing them to one of the iron rings on the wall, and then they left her there in the windowless room, awaiting she knew not what. She could not be sure, but she guessed at the reason that Princess Riedl had summoned her. Hours went by and the candles burned low in the sconces, and Thildin stood against the wall, growing exhausted. Against the paneled wall opposite her stood an altar to the god Bal, the god of pleasure and love. His altar was draped with silk of red and gold. Thildin knew this god was forbidden to the harem. Only Riedl would be privileged enough to secure him a place of worship. As the minutes ticked tediously by and the candlelight grew dim, Thildin gazed at the huge, rigid sex of the god; and though she was limp with weariness, she felt the shell-pink folds of her sex glisten with expectation.

Finally the door opened, and a beautiful woman came in. She had long, curly black hair and skin like milk. Her eyes were large and dark, as luminous as a forest spring in the moonlight. She had the body of a goddess of love, white and firm, each breast standing pert and upright in the silk and leather halter she wore across them. Her legs were long and shapely, and her bottom was round and hard. A tall, brown eunuch accompanied her. As she came through the doorway she pulled away a bit of silk, rubbing her erect nipples between her fingertips; and she came across the room and stood in front of Thildin where she was bound to the wall.

"You are a fine looking woman," said Riedl, "as beautiful as any I have ever seen. Tell me, in following the path of your goddess, do the priestesses of Brida partake in the delights?"

Thildin knew the delights the princess spoke of, for the priestesses of E'Hrglaend were expert in the arts of fertility. Still, she remained silent, feeling unsure, in her degraded condition, in the presence of the assertive princess. The eunuch came to Thildin and took her by the arms. Then Riedl untied Thildin, and Thildin was led to the large bed that stood against the wall and was made to lie down.

"Bind her, Utahr," said Riedl, and the tall dark eunuch reached into a black leather bag that hung from his shoulder pulling out four circlets of leather. With these he tied Thildin's wrists and ankles to the bedposts. Riedl lifted the fine fabric of Thildin's harem skirt, exposing the red hair and the mouth of the hidden love purse between her legs. Thildin shivered with excitement. She began whispering a fervent prayer to Bal that her pleasure, and the pleasure of Princess Riedl, would be accepted as an offering of the finest kind.

Riedl snapped her fingers, signaling to her eunuch.

"The toys," she said.

Uthar reached into the black leather pouch and pulled out three smooth, cylindrical marble objects. They varied in diameter, from very slim to stout, and their colors varied too, from white to pink to brown. As the eunuch pulled out the toys Riedl stared at Thildin, at her large, round breasts, her white thighs, and the thick, dark red hair of her sex.

Princess Riedl began to sort through the smooth marble objects that lay on the bed.

"So, are we ready?" she said to Thildin.

With her finger Riedl probed Thildin's love purse, to check the degree of plumpness that had accrued naturally while she was tied to the wall in the chamber of the god of lust. Princess Riedl was pleased. Thildin's sex had grown juicy and warm indeed.

Princess Riedl spoke to the eunuch in Gosgovnian, which Thildin could only understand partially; but soon she pulled the silk fabric away from Thildin's nipples, and Riedl observed them for readiness before the play could begin.

Riedl found Thildin's nipples to be adequately hard. She climbed up on the bed and began licking the right nipple, encircling and suckling with her pink tongue, until she heard Thildin utter a small gasp of pleasure. Then she sat up and took the slim white piece of marble and began probing gently between the lips of Thildin's sex. She bent over and peered into the sex and worked it ever so carefully, tickling the opening of the cunt until it opened for her in little thrills. Then she picked up the pink marble shaft, which was fatter, and this she pushed inside the wet sex until the shaft was half buried.

Thildin uttered a low moan as the cock-piece entered her cunt.

"Come, you slave. Shed your juices of pleasure in honor of the god Bal!"

Riedl pumped deeper and deeper with the slick pink cock until Thildin was close to climax; but then suddenly Princess Riedl stopped and withdrew the polished cock-piece, which was glistening with the love juices of Thildin's throbbing sex.

Thildin bucked with her hips in little jerks, begging for satisfaction.

"Please, Your Highness, don't stop, don't stop now!"

"That's right," said Riedl. "Beg, or I will leave you here alone to ache for me."

Then Riedl straddled Thildin's face with her thighs and turned her attention to Thildin's swollen love bud. With slow, strong strokes, Riedl licked Thildin's cunt with her tongue. She was pleased when she heard Thildin moan again. Then she began to probe Thildin's love purse with her finger, all the while licking and suckling on her pleasure bud, bringing Thildin close to climax once more. Once she had Thildin moaning and rocking her hips again Riedl parted her legs, pushing her wet cunt down upon Thildin's face to get her pleasure.

"Lick!" she commanded, and Thildin did as she was bid, eagerly stroking Riedl's salty sex with her warm, strong tongue. Soon Riedl was pumping her own pelvis up and down, bringing herself to climax and coming shamelessly without a thought for her unsatisfied slave.

But it was not enough. The slave must come, for the god Bal must be honored. Riedl called out to her eunuch, bidding him to bring her the last toy.

"Bring the brown cock!"

Utahr picked up the brown marble shaft which was the stoutest. Riedl took it from his hand and probed and probed until it sank deeply into Thildin's sex. She pumped it a few times until she heard yet another moan from Thildin. Then she pulled it out of Thildin's pink hole and began probing with her finger in Thildin's brown hole. The brown hole opened quickly, and Riedl was able to push in the brown shaft, pumping slowly and carefully. Then Finally Thildin's cunt yielded, and she came in strong thrusts and shivers.

Afterwards Riedl sat in a comfortable chair and was served wine, and an offering of wine was given to the shrine of Bal, while Thildin was still tied spread-eagled to the bed. Riedl looked at her with satisfaction.

"I am pleased," she said. "I will call you often. Take care not to share yourself with other members of the harem. Your pleasures are for me alone."

With this Riedl left Thildin. Soon the slaves who had brought Thildin arrived, and they tied her again to the wall, while they washed the juices of pleasure from her nether hair. Then they untied her and brought her back to the palace slave quarters where Thildin was left to wonder what else this destiny in Gosgovnia would hold for her.

Chapter 4

In the days before Baeul, Etain spent her time sitting with the king. He loved to sit half naked on his throne while Etain caressed his pendulous jewels and kept his purplish cock standing erect and hard. At times he held her head and brought her willing tongue down over the tip, licking and sucking, to keep the royal sex big and fat and firm. Then, at his leisure, he would command her to lie down on the floor so he could pump her with his engorged member until he came, shedding his seed deep inside her. Until then, he sat on the gilded chair without trousers or loincloth, commanding Etain to keep him ready for as many peaks of pleasure that he could muster.

Etain had grown accustomed to life in the royal palace. The king, though he was a cruel warrior, was kind to her, and quickly he had made her his favorite. In fact, Etain soon learned that King Lasher was fond of his women, and he would not tolerate that any of them should be ill used. Although she must live the life of a slave, Etain found King Lasher's company to be good. She did not have to live in the harem, because the king kept her constantly by his side. This pleased her, for she had heard life in the queen's palace could be tedious. Etain surmised that this was because there was no woman of station to rule it. Queen Elga had died, leaving her young daughter, Riedl, a veritable orphan among the daughters of King Lasher's lesser wives and concubines. It was said that when he and Queen Elga first married, King Lasher had always been with her. By and by, though, he had tired of her, taking other concubines and wives as companions, and Queen Elga had been sent to the harem to live with her small daughter. Still, King Lasher had given Elga dominion over the queen's palace, and Riedl had always been his favorite child.

Now Etain had the king's favor, and she accompanied him everywhere in his palace. They wandered in the long corridors and into every room where King Lasher insisted that Etain lie on the floor and open her legs for lovemaking. While the winter lasted Etain was cloaked in royal blue velvet for excursions into the garden, where he would take her to the flowerbeds, carpeted in snow. There were two rose colored benches there, where guests could sit and admire the garden in the spring, and many was the time King Lasher made Etain kneel upon one of these so he could take her in the cold, spreading the snow-white buttocks to reveal the openings of pink and brown.

Etain counted her blessings, for though there was many a loved one she would never see again, Helkara had been kind to her. Only the thick black collar that King Lasher had fastened around her throat was hard for her to bear. She could try no magic or scrying, for King Lasher kept her leashed with a heavy chain of silver. He would fasten her thus to the wall while he pumped her glistening sex with his cock and probed her tight brown hole with his thumb.

Etain suspected that she was with child, but she had not shared this, not even with her handmaidens. She did not know how King Lasher would take the news, knowing that soon her belly would grow large with pregnancy. She only hoped that pumping her pink hole from behind, and also opening her brown hole, could keep him satisfied until the birth of the child. It was good to be the favorite concubine of the king, to be with him always, while he commanded her incessantly to keep his sex erect. Surely he would bestow a special title upon this child when it was born.

"Come," said the king, "you have been idle far too long. It is time that I pricked you thoroughly. Come and suck me so that I can be hard enough to enter you once again today," said the king.

Etain obeyed. She knelt between the spread knees of the king. With her darting tongue she licked, and then she took the whole cockhead into her mouth for a thorough sucking. The king held her head in his hands and thrust with his pelvis to make her take as much of his penis as she could bear.

"Come, slut, take it, or I will fuck your handmaidens and leave you an unsatisfied old woman," the king cried, as he thrust himself deeper and deeper into her mouth.

But even as a slave, Etain would not tolerate herself to be thus spoken to. The King forgets himself, she thought, speaking so to a high priestess of Brida; and so she stood up from her kneeling position and took the king by the hand.

"Come, sire," she said. "You will never be satisfied until you have tasted the Gate of Life."

It was a bold move. Etain knew the king was not accustomed to any argument, even when he was wrong. But Etain stood steadfastly, courageous even in slavery, for in her person she was a representative of the Goddess. Never could she allow the Triple Goddess to bear such an insult, be she present as Maiden, Mother, or Crone. Quietly she stood above the king, looking down upon him calmly. At first she thought King Lasher might chastise her or strike her, but then she saw with a feeling of righteousness that he was duly humbled.

"Yes, Goddess," he said, "for you, Helkara, are the Giver and Taker of life. You, Helkara, are the Black Angel, who summons the shade of the warrior to the Isle of the Blest."

With that the king knelt at Etain's feet. Gently he caressed her legs, his hands moving upward until his fingers came to rest on her thighs. His strong hands grasped her tightly, and he pulled her to the floor, parting her knees as soon as she lay down. Then tenderly he fingered inside the red hair, until he could part the fat lips of her sex, exposing the wet, shiny pink folds of her cunt. He licked with his tongue, firm, long strokes, until the flower-like opening of the Gate fluttered and parted. His long, probing finger assured him that the Goddess was ready.

Sharply he entered her. Etain rejoiced, for she lay upon a tapestry of the Gosgovnian war god, Balkohr. This meant good fortune for her unborn child, and, after so much licking and sucking, she welcomed the hard, fat cock of the king. Eagerly she spread her legs and parted her cunt lips with her fingers, so that the king would only encounter the wet, hot mouth of her love purse as he thrust and thrust with the thick shaft of his thing. She writhed and gyrated to intensify his pleasure as well as hers, and soon she came, and thereafter he came as well, knowing he had satisfied his slave.

Afterwards Etain retired into her sumptuous quarters where her slaves attended her. She asked leave of the king for a few days, sending him a message that the Goddess required it, and to her surprise he granted her this request. Never before had the king given supremacy to the Goddess over the gods. King Lasher made sure his eunuchs kept Etain leashed and chained; but during this respite Etain savored their last intercourse, planning strategies for pleasuring the king in the days to come.

Chapter 5

Baeul had finally arrived. It was a cool, sunny day. The members of Gol's little household rose early to prepare to go into town, where everyone would celebrate the holiday in the temple square.

This was the day for the charming of the tools, when the Great Goddess Brida was asked for her blessing before the time of the spring planting. Gol loaded a rake, a hoe, trowels, hammers, nails, pots, spoons, harnesses, bits, and even a plough into the back of the cart, which would also be blessed at the ceremony. There would be bonfires as well to cleanse the land after the frozen months of winter.

Olara sat in the wagon seat with Gol and Glendin. She wore a new white linen gown that Glendin had helped her make for the celebration. It was done with needlework at the neckline and on the cuffs of the sleeves, a fine pattern of spring wild flowers. On her feet Olara wore new white sandals of gnoba hide, and across her shoulders she wore a rose colored cloak of wool which kept her warm in the cool spring breeze.

The wagon bumped and rocked as Gol drove the gnoba down the hill away from the farmhouse. Olara found the sensation delicious, for it pressed her against Gol's side. Tonight they would be wed! She tingled as she imagined it, his long, pale fingers on her belly and breasts, pinching and rubbing the nipples that already stood firm, awaiting his loving attention. Then his tongue as he pulled the new white dress away from her eager body, sucking her nipples, licking her navel, down to the curly red hair of her sex, so plump and moist with anticipation. Her wet maidenhead would soften, preparing her cunt folds for penetration. The dull, purplish cockhead that had bobbed upon her belly would rupture her with a single thrust, and she would know the pain of desire satisfied. The gnoba tossed his head and champed his bit, and the tassels on his harness were bright in the morning sun. All around her Olara felt life burgeoning from the earth. The wild flowers, green grass, and singing birds greeted the goddess of the new year, as the crone receded into nature once more.

In the square before the temple of Brida, the citizens of Klaerthelke were gathered. The women and young children were all clad in white, with garlands and ribbons in their hair. They stood in an enormous circle, and the men brought all the tools and stacked them in a great pile, in readiness for the blessing that would come from the high priestess. Gol unloaded the cart and the three of them took their places, waiting for the sacred circle to be drawn.

From the temple doorway the high priestess emerged, and behind her came the rest of the nineteen nuns who served the Virgin Goddess. They carried chalices of gleaming silver filled with pungent red wine, and incense and salt water. The priestess was comely, tall and slender, with a thick plait of light brown hair that hung down upon her snow-white dress. A silver dagger with a jeweled handle hung in a white leather scabbard at her waist. This was the athame, the consecrated knife of magic.

Watching her, Olara felt a pang of sorrow, for it had been but a year since Etain had presided as priestess. She thought of all the loved ones she had lost, whose souls had crossed into the place where the mist meets the sea.

Stillness descended upon the crowd. Attended by two young nuns, the priestess stepped forward and unsheathed her dagger, calling to the powers of the North.

> Hail, Powers of the North
> Dark Mother of the Earth
> Keeper of the Wise Blood and Lady of Winter
> We cast this circle in your name
> And stand within the twilight between the worlds.

With this the priestess raised her knife and traced a pentagram in the air. With the incense and the salt water the attendants purified the direction of the North. The priestess traced an arc with her knife as she moved to the other three cardinal directions, West, South, and East. At each she paused and called out an invocation, and her attendants purified them with the fire of the underworld and the salty water of the womb.

Inside the sacred circle the nuns took the silver chalices of wine, and each member of the community sipped from the sharing cup. The priestess now summoned the gods and goddesses, Brida, Luehg, Hirn, and Daenuhg, and with a branch of evergreen and consecrated water, she blessed the tools that lay in the center of the circle.

Olara stood next to Gol, thinking of the pleasure they would know when darkness fell. She felt impatient as the ceremony drew to a close. Now the people would leave through the city gates. They would meet on the green foothills and there the couples would be wed. Then there would be feasting at long tables laden with food and drink. When the feasting was over, the bonfires would be lit, and Olara and Gol would find a grassy spot in the forest. Olara could think of nothing else as the singing began and the gates of the city opened.

The townspeople met between two grassy knolls, where a Shaeul-n'e-gog had been carved on the face of a great granite monolith. The fertility goddess had enormous, goggling eyes and a huge, lurid grin; and between her parted legs her fingers held open the lips of her life-giving yoni. Now the pairing of the couples would begin.

In two great lines the women stood on one side while the men stood on the other. The married men and women, and all the children and old folk, stood upon the crest of the eastern hill, laughing and telling lewd tales. Then they began to clap their hands and sing a song as old as life. Man and woman, boy and girl, would cleave unto each other on this night and bless the awakening soil with the mingling of their love.

The signal was given and the crowd called out a shout of gladness as the couples reached each other on the green. Gol and Olara held hands and embraced, and then they were carried away, off to the feast on the hillside. Wine, cider, mead, and great platters of meat and pies all lay on the long, wooden tables, awaiting the celebration. Olara ate hungrily, and all the people toasted the brides and brides' grooms, blessing the marriages that would last until next year.

Finally the sun began to set in the west. Upon the crest of the eastern hill stood the great stacks of firewood, and the men of the city assembled there carrying torches to light the bonfires in benediction to the Goddess Brida. Then the bonfires were lit, and the people cheered again. Gol grasped Olara firmly by the wrist. The desire of his body pulsed into hers, and the folds that covered her maidenhead grew wet with anticipation.

The people followed them to the edge of the forest, chanting and singing and clapping their hands. Some of them still held torches to light the way in the darkness. Not a cloud was in the sky, and the three moons of Gwaehr were full and bright and gold. In the blackness the stars twinkled brightly. Surely this night of Baeul was especially blest, and the golden moon goddess lit the path to the groves and anointed the fertile ground.

With the other laughing couples, Olara and Gol ran ahead of the burning torches. Now they must find a hiding place among the ancient evergreens that grew in the forest. With every running step, Olara's happiness grew. She and Gol would be husband and wife, and she would see her sisters again to join in the celebration of life.

As they entered the forest the sound of the crowd receded behind them. Around them they could hear the rustling of the leaves and pine needles as couples everywhere made beds for themselves in the grass; but Gol led Olara ever deeper into the forest, where none would hear them, or be able to tell of the thorough love-making that was in store for her.

Deep, deep into the forest, Gol led Olara to a place that was perfectly still. The moons shone bright and yellow upon them when they finally stopped by the banks of a spring where the trees didn't grow.

"I love this spot in the woods," he said, as Olara stood breathlessly by. "Many are the hours I have spent by this spring. We are alone now, and this is where I will have you, where none may know what we do."

Olara was pleased then, for the spring was an opening into the womb of the Great Mother Goddess. The temple in E'Hrglaend had been built around a spring.

"I am ready," she said, "and my body burns for you."

With that Gol pulled her to the ground and unfastened her cloak. His cock was already fat and firm, eager to rupture her maidenhead. He pushed the snow-white shift up over her breasts, and Olara felt his cool, white hands upon her body. He lay upon her belly and kissed her, and Olara kissed him in return, thrusting her curled, pink tongue into his mouth. His hands pressed her breasts together and he took a nipple into his mouth to suck it. Her legs parted as his hands ran down across her body, into the hair, and he slid a long finger into her wet sex. Slowly and carefully he circled with his finger, pushing against the tender maidenhead, making the love purse ready for the pricking his penis would give her.

Olara's fingers were busy as well. She loosened the drawstring of his trousers, and then she reached in and caught his cock. With one hand she fingered in the curly black hair, and with the other she massaged the shaft of his huge sex. Its skin was supple and hot as she grasped firmly and moved her hand up and down, up and down, until at last she felt a bead of moisture come to the tip. She rubbed the cockhead against her belly and opened her legs, and cried out for Gol to take her.

At the sound of her voice, Gol thrusted his hips and he felt the maidenhead burst. Then he was inside her, and they lay there together very still, now that the long awaited moment had come.

"You will be my wife forever," he said. "Next year we shall wed again, and the next; and then for all the Baeuls to come we will stand with the married folk and sing the praises of the Shaeul-n'e-gog, and together we will see the newly-weds off into the woods."

"And at Ultaine?" Olara said.

"I will have only you," said Gol.

Then Olara's happiness was complete, for this was a promise that would last all their days.

Gol kissed her and smoothed her hair. Then he pushed and prodded with his thick thing, thrusting between her legs inside her hot, wet sex, until finally they both came, and he spent himself deep within her.

Afterwards they kissed and caressed until the three full moons were high in the sky. Then it was time to join the other newly-weds as they left the forest to join the revelers on the hillside. They walked back hand in hand, and all around them they saw the other couples as well, who were all leaving their grassy beds to return home now that spring had been properly ushered in.

The bonfires still glowed red and hot when Olara and Gol reached the edge of the forest. Glendin was there with a great flagon of mead, talking with the other wise women of the town. Gol was pleased to see his mother enjoying herself. Life would be better for her with a new daughter-in-law. Soon there would be grandchildren playing in the house, for surely Olara would bear him many children.

As the bonfires burned out, the townspeople began to walk back to the city. Lighting their way with torches the men gathered up the tools from the temple square, and everyone trundled off to bed. Gol loaded the wagon and harnessed the gnoba who tossed his head in anticipation of a late supper of grain and hay when he returned to the stable. It had been a long, wonderful day, and tomorrow they would rest.

As Olara sat in the wagon seat next to Gol, she thought of her sisters and wondered what had become of them. How had this holiday passed for them? Surely they still lived and had been taken to Gosgovnia, far away across the sea. She prayed to Helkara that their captors were treating them as befitted their high station, and that they were not suffering for lack of drink and nourishment. She remembered the hard winter she had spent as a beggar in Klaerthelke, without food or shelter, or proper clothing to keep her warm. Were her sisters suffering so? Her own training in magic and scrying had been ended when the war was lost, but Etain and Thildin were masters in all the arts of the temple. Were they trying to reach her, or had their captors kept them from the implements they needed to practice the crafts they knew so well?

These questions nagged her as her new family made its way back home. They would not come back to town tomorrow, but in the days to come Olara would accompany Gol with his merchant's cart, now that she was his new wife. If Etain and Thildin were free, they surely would have come to her by now. Perhaps there was no one, no one else but she, a fledgling novitiate without the slightest knowledge of medicine or magic; but somehow she must gain the power to face the Gosgovnians, or her sisters would never be free. She would go with Gol into Klaerthelke, and though she knew that revealing her true heritage could endanger her newfound happiness, she resolved to speak to the offworlders who came to Gol's cart to buy.

Chapter 6

It was Baeul. The day of the public deflowering of Etain had arrived. Although she was certain that she already carried the seed of the king in her womb, still, under Gosgovnian law, Etain was considered virgin until this public ritual had been observed. Etain had almost grown accustomed to her collar and chain, and without doubt she now welcomed the carnal attentions of her master; for King Lasher was well endowed and lascivious by nature, and their encounters grew more sensual and wanton with each passing day.

Sometimes Etain thought of the life she once knew, pristine and unsampled, virgin, high priestess, and abbess of the most powerful society in the land of the E'Hrglaends. Now she was but a toy, a morsel of flesh to be savored and consumed, her entire existence turning merely on the appetite of her master; but Etain knew that this was the way of the Goddess, and that the mighty might ever be brought low.

For many weeks Etain had anticipated this day with apprehension, for she knew not what to expect. She only knew that there would be hundreds of people watching as she was led onto a great wooden platform in the town square of Gelstohr. There King Lasher would bare her puff of red hair and her secret cleft, and plunge and thrust with his fat, mighty penis, until she writhed and pitched for all to see.

Her preparation for this event had begun early, for King Lasher had not visited her person for thirteen days. She was fed special foods, rich meats and sauces, and strong mead spiced with herbs that enhanced animal desire. She was closely watched and chained, and the eunuchs who attended her saw to it that she finished everything she was brought to eat, for she would in no way escape the artifice and will of the king.

While her mind was prepared for the spectacle, her body was prepared as well. Every morning she was taken naked to the slave's chambers, and there female slaves bound her wrists to an iron ring in the wall. Then she was carefully washed and massaged. Special attention was paid to her sex which was probed with sponges drenched in scented water. When this was done the slaves fastened a small clamp of carved ivory onto her pleasure bud. Then they pumped her pink hole and her brown hole vigorously with fat cocks of polished cedar until Etain reached the pitch of pleasure; but always they stopped, leaving Etain's cunt aching with desire.

This ritual was performed three times a day in the period that King Lasher was absent from her, and the two brawny eunuchs who attended her made sure that she did not satisfy herself with her fingers in between; for Etain's wrists were kept tightly bound before her in nooses of thick black leather, which were only untied at meal time so she could feed on the sumptuous delicacies.

And so Etain was prepared for the king's great day. At night, chained to her bed, she could not even think of her magic. She could only think of the king's fat cock and hanging testicles and the fine pricking he would give her in front of the crowd.

On the morning of Baeul her female slaves came to her bedchamber, for now the final preparations would begin. They carried a dressing gown of white silk embroidered with birds and flowers. This they put on her person before they led her from her room to the chamber of the virgins.

It was a large room with gleaming mahogany paneling, as in other parts of the palace. It was bare of furniture except for a great wardrobe of glazed cedar which had two large drawers. On each side of the room the walls had been fitted with iron rings. There Etain saw other slaves, beautiful princesses from conquered provinces, who would also be deflowered on the platform. They, like she, wore collars, and they had also been clothed in white silk gowns; but now they stood naked, their wrists bound before them to the iron rings in the wall while their gowns of silk lay folded behind them in a great pile on the floor.

Etain knew that these slaves would be taken before her and deflowered on the platform in groups of two or three. They would be given to deserving vassals of the king, or perhaps to a warrior who had shown exceptional bravery and cunning on the battlefield. There were twelve other slaves beside her, for even among the Gosgovnians, the number sacred to the Goddess was thirteen.

Two black eunuchs stood watch at the door while the female attendants were busy preparing the slaves. Some of the slaves stood quietly while they were washed and massaged and anointed, but others whimpered and cried piteously, unable to accept their fate fearlessly. Some of them, Etain knew, had never known cock and balls, and for these it seemed to Etain that their destiny was harsh indeed.

Now Etain's attendants led her to the wall to be bound there to the iron ring. With her hands above her head Etain waited while the ritual bathing began. As before she was carefully washed, every inch of her skin. Then she was commanded to spread her legs so that attention could be given to her sex. With a soft piece of gnoba suede the slaves rubbed and washed, rubbed and washed, removing the juices of desire that were already moistening Etain's pink cunt and pleasure bud. Then, when the washing was finally through, the slaves took soft cloths of Vasquhnian cotton and carefully dried the sex and the puff of red hair that was the king's pride.

Then Etain was anointed with fine, scented oil from the province of Brokahn. Behind her she could hear the crying of the other slaves while the perfume of the oil filled her nostrils and made her giddy, as much as if she had drunk a goblet of sweet wine. The slave girls spread the oil on every inch of Etain's skin, rubbing and massaging, but the tension in Etain's body was ever mounting as she anticipated the moment to come.

At last, when the oiling was complete, the slave girls attended to her sex once more. They dipped their fingers into the Brokahnian oil, and slowly they oiled the sex, circling and fingering, until Etain felt her love cleft fatten and her nether juices flowing once more. Then a touch of perfumed powder was applied to the puff of red hair, and Etain was ready to be dressed.

All around her the attendants had washed and oiled and perfumed the other twelve slaves. Now the slaves were untied from the iron rings that held their wrists above their heads in preparation to be robed. The two black eunuchs stood guard at the doorway, each one of them brandishing a long, black leather strap that could be used to cow any princess who might think of disrupting decorum.

Now the garments for the captives were brought forth. The breast binders were beautiful, rich velvet worked with thread of silver and gold. As Etain watched the first princesses being dressed, she saw that these were mere halters, exposing the breast mounds and also the fat nipples. All the slaves were bound in these brief garments, while their legs and nether hair remained exposed. A halter-brassiere was also fastened on Etain, sharply pressing her breasts until they stood out in high, snowy mounds. Etain looked down and saw her hard nipples, just waiting to be taken into the mouth of a man.

For a moment Etain feared they would be led out onto the platform with nothing to cover their nakedness except the tight halters; but then the attendants reached back into the great wardrobe and brought out translucent harem skirts for each of the slaves to wear. Etain was familiar with the design. They were made of filmy fabric of silver and gold, with a triangular band of worked velvet that hung upon the hips. There were four straight panels, two in front and two in back, so that the legs of the slaves could be seen from the side. More ingenious, the panels could be lifted from the front and back, so that the sex of the slave was available from both the front and behind.

The garments were quite transparent, and in the morning light Etain could clearly see the nether hair that belonged to each slave. And so they would be nearly naked, she thought, when they mounted the platform before the crowd in the bright sunshine.

The attendants fitted Etain with her harem skirt. It had panels of translucent gold that hung from a triangle of embroidered velvet of forest green. This matched the green velvet halter that pushed her breasts up high. The green was especially beautiful in contrast to her long, red hair, and the puff of her sex was even more visible through the filmy skirt than it was on the other princesses, because of its brilliant color.

Now the slaves were to be rouged. The attendants went into the large drawers of the great wardrobe and pulled out fat sticks of red wax softened with perfumed oil. Then they went to the slaves and colored their nipples that stood high above their tight brassieres. They massaged the color in carefully, making every nipple, be it pink or brown, into a small, hard pebble of scarlet. In this way they assured that the expectant crowd would be able to appreciate every dainty detail of the beautiful princesses.

Next it was time to rouge the sex of each slave. The attendants commanded the captives to spread their legs. Then the attendants squatted on the floor, peering directly into the hostage's love clefts. Carefully they circled the cunts with the soft red wax, until each love purse was a bright, glistening crimson. The crowd would be well pleased with this harvest of feminine royalty. It was almost time for the ceremony to begin.

Etain had been rouged, both cunt and nipples, just like the other slaves. She had born this travail with surprising ease, and the fat, red pencil of wax had made her more desirous of the cocking that was to come.

It was time. The attendants stood back while the slaves that still whimpered were paddled thrice for their cowardice. There would be no display of sorrow or distress on the platform, for the princesses existed now purely for the satisfaction of their new masters.

The eunuchs accompanied them with their attendants as the slaves were led down a dark, narrow hallway, to a great mahogany door that opened through the outer wall of the palace. Outside the sunlight was so bright that Etain squinted her eyes. Immediately they were met with cheering and laughter from hundreds of people who lined up along the cobbled road that led from the palace to the town. Etain was very conscious of the translucency of her gown, and the sight her red puff must be making for the crowd, as the princesses were herded down the stone path and into a crude wooden cart drawn by a team of sleek, snow-white gnobi. Then down the cobbled path they rattled, as the jeering throng closed ranks and followed them from behind.

The journey to the platform seemed endless, but at last Etain saw it, standing thirty feet tall. It was covered with a huge, creamy white tapestry wrought with blood red flowers. Upon a second stage that stood on the western border of the square Etain could see King Lasher seated in a great golden chair. The eunuchs drove the slaves out of the cart with their long leather paddles into a gated pavilion where they could see the platform clearly. All around her Etain could see the round, firm buttocks and high white breasts of the young princesses. She was grateful that they were placed at a distance from the excited townspeople, and that none were allowed to touch or harass them while they waited to meet their destiny.

The spectacle was mastered by a tall, burly man with a staff who wore a long white cloak and hood. He stood in the center of the stage before the noisy crowd, and his presence alone quieted the clamoring while everyone waited for the ceremony to begin. Then he raised his staff high in the air, and a giant roar emanated from the throng, for now the celebrations would commence.

A slave came to the gate of the pavilion and handed one of the eunuchs a scroll of parchment. The eunuch frowned, attempting to read the scarlet script in the sunlight.

"Bring the slaves Heldah, Elmora, and Sylnina," he said in a loud, commanding voice.

The masses of people before the platform went wild. The other eunuch opened the gate and swung his black leather strap. To the sound of the roars and cheers the first three princesses, two lovely brunettes and a blonde beauty, were driven out of the pavilion. Although their hearts might have been quaking at the ordeal they must face, yet they made not a sound, in fear of the thick black lash. They were marched to the platform, and there they climbed a flight of wooden stairs. Etain could see them well from where she stood, and she saw that their buttocks and legs, as well as their dark mounds of nether hair, could be seen clearly by all. Etain felt a shiver run over her body, and an aching began that started deep in her cunt and flowed to the insides of her thighs.

Finally they reached the top of the platform. Etain could see that from the opposite side three men had mounted the stairs. They were dressed in bronze armor, each with a sword and strap swinging at their hips. They made a grand show of themselves with their two hands fisted together above their heads. Again a roar rose from the crowd. The eunuchs pushed the princesses towards the center of the platform. Then there came a booming voice from the tall, hooded master of the stage, as he raised his staff high over his head.

"A fine cocking for the slave Elmora, princess of the conquered land of Bazul; from Fornkohr the Black, who has been a true and brave servant of King Lasher! May he fuck her deeply, and may she shed her cunt juices on this fine Baeul day!"

Etain felt her legs quivering at the sound of the hooded man's voice and the lips of her sex grow fat and wet as the aching continued in her cunt. The vassal Fornkohr the Black took the princess by her collar, and led her to the edge of the stage. There he made her face front and center, so that the crowd could appreciate her beauty. He pulled the tight halter down so that the breasts popped out over the top, leaving the scarlet nipples standing erect. As the crowd hooted and called he turned her around and pulled up her harem skirt, baring her bottom to the world. He made her lie down and open her legs, and with the big, stiff strap he parted the lips of her sex, exposing the brightly rouged cunt to the throng. As the cheering and roaring rose he took her by the collar and pulled her to her feet. Then with his thick black stick he prodded her behind, making her hop and trot before him as they moved across the stage.

Etain's apprehension grew as she watched the spectacle on the platform. Would King Lasher, her kind master, submit her, too, to this grisly ordeal? The tension in her body mounted as the other two slaves were handed off to their new masters and exhibited before the crowd; but still she felt the ache of pleasure glowing in her pink hole, as she waited for the fucking to begin.

All three slaves now stood at their masters' sides, docile as lambs. The white robed master gave the signal, raising his staff high. At once the new slave owners threw off their weapons and loosened the drawstrings of their trousers. Three big, fat cocks came into view, and there was another round of cheering from the crowd. The princesses were commanded to get down on the tapestry, the brunettes on their backs, and the blonde on her hands and knees. Then the men went to work on them, plunging and thrusting into the virginal holes, cock and cunt coming together in a splendid celebration of the year's first union of Goddess and God. The spectacle of the blonde was especially exciting to the crowd, for her master cocked her from behind, all the while giving her brown hole a good plugging with his thumb. With their fat penises the masters worked the slaves relentlessly, until all three princesses convulsed with pleasure before the eyes of the townspeople; and the spent juices of their lust assured the fertility of the land.

Etain's anxiety grew as she watched the new couples descend the wooden stairs to make way for the next venue. She dared not make a sound, in fear of incurring the stern discipline of the eunuch's strap, but she wrung her hands together and felt that her palms had grown cold and clammy. Her skin tingled and prickled while her cunt still ached with desire. Her heart pumped madly in her breast, and she heard the din of the masses as if from a dream world. Her command of meditation had once given her the power to change a blossom to a stone; but now she could not calm herself in the least as she perpended the inevitable moment of Fate that awaited her.

She heard the eunuch read the names off the roster; Janzah, Kritania, Pelopa; Carlina, Wendoline, Enchopah; Maerkona, Phillomina, Neldora. Three by three the princesses were driven from the pavilion with the great leather strap, and three by three they mounted the wooden staircase to meet their masters. Although Etain could hardly bear to watch, yet her cunt ached and her eyes were riveted to the stage; and the spectacle of each perfect nipple, and each fat, glistening love bud, was etched into her mind as with fire.

And then the moment came when the union of slave and master was complete, and the stage stood empty, awaiting the greatest venue; for now King Lasher himself would take a bride, and publicly the dull head of his cock would open her, pledging his body and his get to the people and the land.

"Bring the slave Etain!" cried the eunuch.

She could hardly recognize her name; but the gate of the pavilion swung open, and with the stiff strap Etain was coaxed outside its sanctuary. At a trot the eunuch drove her up the staircase and onto the great stage where she could see King Lasher walking up the steps on the other side. The color rose to her face as she felt a sea of eyes behold every detail of her nakedness.

The roar of the crowd was deafening when King Lasher stepped onto the fine tapestry that covered the stage. He was dressed in his royal armor, and at his hips Etain could see his sword and black leather strap. The white robed master himself took Etain by the collar and led her to front and center where the people could begin to appreciate this fine prize. Then he raised his staff high and called out for all to hear.

"A fine cocking for the slave Etain, high priestess of the conquered land of E'Hrglaend; from King Lasher the Mighty, who has been a true and brave servant of the people of Gosgovnia. May he fuck her deeply, and may she shed her cunt juices on this fine Baeul day!"

A cry of victory filled Etain's ears as King Lasher moved to the center of the stage. It resonated in the very air and sent chills of passion vibrating through her bones.

"Long live King Lasher! Long live King Lasher! Long live King

Lasher!"

Her lord and master now stood before her, and he was comely in his royal armor of polished bronze. Etain looked at him beseechingly, and felt the aching in her cunt intensify.

But the king did not take her by the collar. He only stood quietly, tapping his thigh with his stiff black strap; and Etain found herself walking towards him, coming to him of her own free will.

When she reached him, the king took her gently by the hand. He did not pull on the tight halter to expose her breasts, but merely pinched and massaged the rouged nipples instead.

The king threw off his sword and trousers. There was more cheering as he paraded his stiff, engorged penis before the crowd. At first Etain thought she might escape the unveiling of her rouged cleft; but the scarlet sex must be exhibited before the people, who were awaiting the climax of this fine holiday.

The king commanded Etain to get down on her hands and knees with her bottom facing the crowd. Etain quaked with anxiety as she awaited what she knew must follow. With his stiff stick the king lifted the sheer panels of her skirt, and Etain could hear the hooting and calling that rose from the masses at the sight of her white buttocks. Still Etain was hopeful that this was all she would have to endure; but instead King Lasher spread her buttocks wide, and the people went wild as the aching, hidden holes of scarlet and brown were unveiled to them.

Now the moment of the opening had come. King Lasher commanded Etain to turn herself so that she could be seen in profile. Then he mounted her from behind, plunging the blunt head of his hard prick deep inside her throbbing cunt, knocking against her seeded womb. Sharply he thrusted, over and over, until suddenly the throbbing was too great; and Etain felt the spasms of pleasure undulate from the depths of her cleft and ripple through her soul.

But King Lasher had not finished with Etain, for now he withdrew his penis, dripping with the juices of passion. He poised his cock for the opening of the brown hole. The prick head battered and went in, and Etain uttered a low moan as the king plunged his huge, fat shaft deep into the brown flower. Eagerly he pumped and thrusted while he spread Etain's legs to finger and pinch her engorged love bud; and again Etain felt the throbbing waves of pleasure, and she shed her cunt juices once more.

And so the public opening was done, and Etain was virgin no more. Forever she was bound to the king as the king was bound to the land; and for all her days she would serve the face of Helkara, the Dark Mother who is the womb of life.

Chapter 7

In the queen's chamber, Princess Riedl sat alone. She gazed out of the window, brooding, watching the king's gardeners as they toiled in the spring sunshine.

The splendor of the mighty Gosgovnian Empire surrounded her in this room, a room that her father had arrayed especially for her mother. The finest creations of Gosgovnian artisans were to be found here. On the walls there were the customary Gosgovnian tapestries, crafted in intricate patterns depicting the gods and men; but there was captured booty, too, objects of beauty the war-like Gosgovnians had never mastered on their own. The chairs were upholstered in violet silk from the province of Beltonia, the scented candles on the walls came from Harkohn. There were gilded mirrors that were made in the land of the Vasquhnians, and delicate arrangements of crystals and gems that imitated the wild flowers of the valleys of Kahltoon. From every corner of the known world of Gwaehr there were objects of imagination and ingenuity, created for the sole purpose of pleasing the eye; and here the princess was wont to while away the time, with no community of fellowship save her own.

Riedl, the favorite of her father, enjoyed considerable luxury in the harem. She was even favored above her half-brother, Ahtaar, the son of King Lasher's second wife. Although this younger brother was the king's rightful heir, it was Riedl that he had taken on his knee. It was well known in all of Gosgovnia that nearly every wish of the Princess Riedl was her father's command, nearly every one, except the wish to be free.

Riedl was stifled by harem life. In another land her intelligence and diligence might have made her a priestess or a saint, but in Gosgovnia she led the life of a privileged slave. It was true her father had seen to it that she learned to read and write, and she was allowed to keep books, which was a privilege she shared with no other woman in Gosgovnia; but the princess yearned for more. She knew not even what it was she missed. She only knew her life was dull and incomplete.

Princess Riedl looked about her in the elegant room that was the queen's chamber. Her earliest memories of her mother were in this room. Queen Elga had died when Riedl was only five; but Riedl cherished her still, and was sure that it was here that her mother continued to be near her.

Queen Elga had been a foreigner, but a woman of noble birth. Her union with King Lasher had been arranged, purely a political contract; but the marriage had been, for Elga, a true love match; that is, until the king had tired of her. Now the priestess Etain had the favor of the king. Princess Riedl felt no bitterness or jealousy towards Etain, for she guessed that even her mother had been suffocated by these walls, and she sometimes wondered if perhaps Queen Elga had died of a broken heart.

Riedl's beauty was renowned throughout her father's kingdom, and she had had many suitors; but the king had never consented to a marriage. This was of no importance to the princess, for she had no interest in being a wife. In Gosgovnia all women were powerless, and to Riedl men existed only to be manipulated to obtain her own ends.

Riedl tired of her father's endless war campaigns, for secretly she had read stories of people who revered peace; but her father's last conquest had brought her Thildin, and for this she was very glad.

Riedl had grown fond of Thildin. Thildin was eleven winters older than the princess, and though Thildin was her slave, Riedl looked up to her, for she was trained in the ways of the wise woman. Riedl had chosen her as a teacher so that she, too, might in some way follow the Path. She was fascinated by the religion of the E'Hrglaendi, where the Goddess was served before the gods.

And so Riedl's slaves brought Thildin to the chamber of Bal nearly every day, but not all their hours there were occupied with play. Riedl pressed Thildin for knowledge, always wanting to hear more, in every subject that pertained to the secret knowledge of the temple of Brida. Headache remedies, cures for toothaches, and the special herbs used for the alleviation of the pains of childbirth, as well as poultices to heal wounds and to stop bleeding, were all topics of interest. Then on other days Thildin lectured on magic, to cast a love spell, to hex an enemy with the Evil Eye, and to sing the invocations of the days that were holy to the greater and lesser gods and goddesses. As the time passed, Riedl's knowledge and her love of Thildin grew; but she told no one of her studies, fearing that her father would learn of them.

Thildin's great beauty also drew Riedl to her. Her fiery hair and snow-white skin enchanted and excited her. As she looked out the window upon the royal gardens she thought of Thildin's firm breasts and exquisite pink nipples. Riedl had spent hours with Thildin as her bedfellow. She loved to play Thildin's favorite games with the eunuch Utahr attending. How compliant Thildin had grown when Riedl commanded her to part her legs and bare her sex for pleasure. Tying and chaining were no longer required, though at times it was still implemented in the spirit of fun. As she thought of it Riedl felt the folds of her own sex moisten and soften with anticipation. Today she would call upon Thildin again, and she resolved to give her a pricking with a big, black cock of polished ebony.

Riedl commanded and Thildin obeyed, for Riedl was mistress and Thildin was slave; but Riedl wanted more than this. She wanted to win Thildin's affection. It was partly for this that Riedl was so diligent in her studies of magic and medicine. And there was something else that Riedl did, which would have angered her father, had he known. Riedl had told Thildin that Etain was now the primary consort of the king, for she could not bear to see her fret over her lost sisters. She had also promised to supply Thildin with everything she needed to scry and to perform minor spells. In this way she hoped to gain Thildin's approval, for Riedl saw in Thildin a means to her own spiritual liberation, and for this she would put even her life at stake.

*　　　　　　　*　　　　　　　*

Thildin awaited the Princess Riedl, attended by handmaidens and slaves. Two brawny eunuchs, both black as midnight, stood at the draped doorway that led into the paneled corridor of tapestries. It must be nearly time, thought Thildin impatiently, for the princess to summon her to their romp. With anticipation she thought of what Princess Riedl would have in store for her today. At every meeting Riedl had surprised her with ever more inventive erotic play, and the priestess, who had once thought herself seasoned in the arts of fertility, was amazed at the ingenuity of this harem girl.

And today was particularly special, for Riedl had promised her that after their lark she would be given the opportunity to scry and cast a spell for the Seeing Eye. Riedl had been good to Thildin. Since Thildin now knew that Etain was alive and safe, she would concentrate on finding Olara.

Finally the slaves who were wont to escort her to the princess entered through the draped doorway and summoned her to come. As they walked through the great hallway hung with tapestries Thildin felt her excitement grow.

Princess Riedl awaited her in the windowless chamber, and the eunuch Utahr was with her. Upon the altar of Bal Riedl had already placed a sacrifice of mead and red wine. A table had been placed next to the altar. Thildin saw a great crystal bowl filled with water, and dishes of the herbs and plants she would need to work the spell for the Seeing Eye. The candles in the room were all burning bright, and Utahr carried the black leather bag that Thildin had come to know so well.

Riedl came to her and kissed her, a long, delicious kiss of greeting.

"I've done as I said I would," she said. "I've gathered the things you've asked for, and when we're through playing you promised to teach me the art of scrying."

Thildin moved to the table in her beautiful costume and saw that all the implements were there. She turned to Riedl, smiling a smile of true affection and appreciation. In that moment, her respect for Riedl grew, for Thildin knew what risk the princess was taking, and just how much she had to lose.

Now the time for play had come. Riedl commanded Thildin to lie down on the bed. Thildin obeyed, parting her legs to uncover her shell-pink love purse that lay hidden beneath her thick bush of red hair.

Riedl went to the altar of Bal and kneeled in supplication. In her studies of the religion of E'Hrglaend, she had not forgotten the gods of her own people. She bowed her head, asking for a blessing for this day's sensuous union.

Thildin asked to be tied. Without a word, Utahr did as he was bid. Out of his bag he pulled two circlets of black leather. He slipped them over Thildin's hands, and bound her wrists to the bedposts.

Upon the table next to the scrying bowl stood a flask of red wine and a beautifully enameled saucer laden with sea salt. Riedl took up the flask and saucer and carried them to the bedside where Utahr stood ready with his pouch of black leather.

"Thildin," said Riedl, "you have been very bad. You were not ready when my slaves came to summon you. For this you must be punished." Then she looked up at Utahr and said, "Bind her!"

Utahr reached into his bag, and wordlessly he pulled out two more circlets of leather. Thildin was docile as he slipped the thongs over her ankles and tied her feet to the bedposts.

Riedl threw back the hem of Thildin's harem skirt and tugged upon the fabric of her brassiere. Now Thildin's nipples were nicely exposed, as well as her thighs and the opening of her sex. Riedl took the flask and trickled the wine over Thildin's breasts, across the center of her chest and down to the hollow of her navel. She pinched the wine stained nipples, over and over again, until Thildin winced.

"Bad slave," she said, "Bad, bad slave!"

Then she sucked and licked, stroking with her tongue until she reached the little pool of wine in Thildin's navel. Riedl lapped that up, too, and then she sat up and scowled at Thildin.

"You wretched slave, you have ruined your beautiful gown! For this you must be punished!"

Then she took a bit of sea salt between her fingers and rubbed them into Thildin's sensitive nipples. The salt stung after the sucking the princess had given them, and Thildin responded with sharp cries that could not be distinguished from the cries of pleasure. Riedl took more and more of the sea salt, rubbing it on Thildin's breasts and belly as she had done with the wine. Then she licked the salt off of the nipples, in preparation for the final tableau of the trial.

"She has ruined her gown, she must be punished," cried Riedl. "Utahr, the whip."

Utahr reached into his black bag, and pulled out a whip of knotted thongs that had been lashed to a bone handle.

"Whip her," Riedl cried. "Whip the ungrateful slave!"

With that Utahr gave a lashing to the lips of Thildin's sex, thirteen strokes in all; but Thildin's travail had yet to end.

Riedl parted the wounded lips of Thildin's sex so that the opening of her love purse was nicely exposed. Then she dipped her slender finger into the sea salt, and carefully rubbed it into the glistening cunt. Thildin squealed and squealed, but Riedl kept rubbing with her finger, around the opening of the sex, while her own cunt folds grew hot and wet with pleasure.

"It is done. You have atoned for your sins," Riedl said at last. Then she licked the sea salt from the sex, stroking and probing with her tongue, into the mouth of the hole.

But Riedl wasn't finished yet, for now Utahr pulled the big ebony cock from his bag. Its polished surface gleamed in the candlelight. Riedl pushed her bottom into Thildin's face and commanded her to lick. Then she gave Thildin a thorough pricking with the ebony cock until both of them came and were satisfied.

Afterwards the women rested and talked, and enjoyed goblets of heady red wine. Thildin was allowed to make an offering of a scented candle to the god Bal.

"And now," said Thildin, "I will be mistress, for you have promised me the chance to scry."

She stood up and went to the table where the magical materials were assembled. First she picked up a sprig of sage and prepared to smudge the room, to remove all harmful influences before she cast the sacred circle. From the scented candle that burned on the altar of Bal she lit the tip of the sage, creating a thin ribbon of aromatic smoke that drifted towards the ceiling. Then she walked around the circumference of the room, dipping with the sprig of sage, until the chamber was perfumed with the sweet-smelling smoke and the smudging was complete. She took incense and salt water and purified the four directions, north, east, south, and west, invoking the powers of earth, air, fire, and water; and the sacred circle was drawn.

Thildin placed the bowl of water on the floor in the middle of the room. She took white petals of lindl blossoms, and sprinkled them on the floor around the bowl. She instructed Riedl to light more incense and to extinguish the tapers that burned on the wall. Riedl did as she was bid, leaving only the candle on the altar burning. Darkness descended on the room, except for the glow that emanated from the single flickering flame.

The room was now a chamber of midnight. The flame of the candle was reflected in the dark water of the scrying bowl. Thildin concentrated and gazed upon it, knowing the hour of magic had come.

Minutes passed, and Riedl stood breathlessly by as Thildin murmured an ancient prayer to the Great Seeing Eye. The facets of the crystal bowl gleamed in the candlelight, and the dark water rippled as Thildin let fall the crumbled blossoms of the lindl tree. The ripples receded, and she meditated upon the reflection of the flickering flame, waiting, waiting for an image to appear to her on the surface of the water. Again and again she whispered the age-old invocation, petitioning the Crone who held the Seeing Eye over the blood filled cauldron of the Dark Mother, the Grinning Goddess whose gaping yoni was the gate to both womb and tomb.

Thildin felt the veil of the mysteries descend upon her. Her limbs and chest grew heavy, but she could hear the chanting of the invocation, filling the space around her as if it came from the voices of a hundred dead children instead of from her own heaving breast. Rising, the voices carried her upward, until she saw herself from a great distance sitting before the crystal bowl, the flickering reflection of the flame ever before her eyes. The chanting droned in her ears. Upward and outward she spiraled, the veil expanding with her, until she felt her soul body engulf the entire room. The candlelight infused her with a warm, gentle energy, and the smell of the sage was sweet in her nostrils. She felt the power of the sacred circle around her, and the veil, and the minutes ticked by as she hovered there, watching the forms of herself, Riedl, and Utahr as they gathered around the scrying bowl. Keenly she felt the veil, the misty boundary between the spirit world and the world of the living. The chanting swelled around her, as spirit voices and the voices of the dead rose from the black waters of the Abyss and called upon the Seeing Eye. They called out with her in a rhythmic, pulsing song. The power of the spell grew as she drew their shades to her, beckoning them to cross over the veil, commanding them into the center of the sacred circle, adding their forces to the energy of her own soul body. She felt the room filled with the potency of their beings. Now she had generated the heart of a new temple, and the power of the Seeing Eye would be with her soon.

The eyes of her soul body hovered beneath the veil. The singing of the invocation grew distant to her ears. Before her the images of the room, of Riedl and Utahr and her own body, gave way to great vistas of plains and mountains and seas. Valleys and cities passed beneath her. Then she was on the shoreline of the Bridin Sea, racing with the night wind eastward, the crashing of the waves rising with the singing voices of the cold Abyss. Outward over the ocean she spun, speeding northward across the sea, the three moons of Gwaehr shining brightly above her, the dark waters of the great womb of the earth beneath her. She could feel the wind ripple through her, and rays of starlight shone from her heart and glittered in her limbs and her hair. As a twinkling specter she was blown northward by the ocean wind, far out over the Bridin Sea, racing over the surface of the water, onward and onward to the shores of the north and the lost homeland of E'Hrglaend.

She had almost reached her destination. Ahead of her in the glow of the moonlight she could see the white-capped waves of the E'Hrglaendi shore. She could hear the surf rolling onto the sand, and the shoreline of white sand was silver beneath the night sky, stretching away from her to the east and west like a great white serpent slithering away behind the horizon. Deeply the voices of the dead droned on, singing the age-old spell in rhythm with the pounding waves on the shoreline, leading her soul body to the base of the craggy black cliffs overlooking the Bridin Sea.

And then she was home once more, and she saw her father's castle in the moonlight, standing as it had stood for three hundred years before the Gosgovnian invasion. Everything was peaceful and still, and she longed for the spirits to lead her inside to see the home fires burning, to sit just one more time with the loved ones who had passed away from the living, beyond the veil of the Mysteries, and into the place where the mist meets the sea.

But then the veil contracted and her soul body with it, spiraling her downward to the plane of chanting, down into the center of the temple she had created in the chamber of Bal. Again she felt the candlelight infuse her, and the smell of the sage was sweet in her nostrils, and she saw herself once more sitting before the bowl of crystal, the fragrant lindl petals falling from her hand. For a moment she hovered there, high above Riedl and her own kneeling form. Then with a rush she was on the surface of the dark water, and the reflected candle flame burst upon her consciousness as her soul body returned to her physical form.

Now the chanting came from her own voice once more, and her breathing came deeply and slowly as she absorbed the power in the room. One, two, three, she chanted in rhythm to her heartbeat, and the power pulsed into the blood of her veins, coursing from her heart to the great blood filled cauldron and back again.

Then, slowly, unformed at first, the images started to appear to her on the water's dark surface. There were colors and shapes all a blur, flowing one into the other, and a deafening roaring sound came to Thildin's ears, so that she could not hear herself chanting the age-old spell. Faces flashed by her eyes, contorted in anguish and fear. And then it opened up and she saw the Bridin countryside all a flame, people running and falling in a hail of Gosgovnian arrows, the blood seeping into the soil, the screams of the wounded and dying piercing her to the heart. Then she saw a farmhouse with a wife and four small children. They begged for their lives, but the soldiers barred the door and cast flaming torches upon the dry roof of thatch. Then there was nothing but the roaring of fire and the soldiers standing and watching as their victims burned alive inside.

Fire, everywhere fire. She saw a barn, and inside the bodies of twenty-three young men and boys where they had been hanged from the rafters, their faces blue and bloated, before the Gosgovnians set the building ablaze while they drank from their gnoba skin bags.

Then she saw what she only too clearly knew from memory. Fifty of them had barricaded themselves inside the main hall of the castle in a hopeless attempt to avoid the warriors' wrath. The men and boys, holding the barred door, while the women and children huddled together against the far wall of the room. But the door could not be held. With axes and battering rams the Gosgovnians burst in. The women screamed as the men and babies were put to the sword. She herself was taken prisoner, and the more beautiful women as well, but even most of the women were not spared death. They were raped, and then their throats were cut, their bright blood covering the floor. She saw the murder of her white haired father as he was bludgeoned and beaten by the soldiers, who finally dealt him his deathblow with a warrior's axe which split his skull. Twitching, he lay in the blood of his brain, which matted his hair and congealed in a great bright red pool around him. A shudder passed through her, knowing she would see him no more. Then she saw the countryside, the fire and the dead lying where they had fallen, and a few miserable prisoners who were tied and prodded with the hilts of swords as the victorious Gosgovnians made their way back to the beach. The carnage was ended. She had seen the land purified of all that was mortal, the Dark Mother taking unto her all that was Her due.

Then the waters grew quiet. Thildin, much moved by what she had seen, fought to hold her concentration, to accomplish the task she had set out to do. The pictures swirled and faded. The water cleared and for an instant she saw the face of Etain, sleeping soundly by King Lasher's side. Then the water rippled and grew dark again. Thildin struggled to keep focus, concentrating on the reflection of the candle. Finally a glazed image began to appear. It was the likeness of a woman's face, a face that Thildin held dear.

She saw her sister Olara, dwelling above a mountain city, and by her side there was a fair skinned man with dark curly hair. Her sister lived, and she was free. Thildin could hardly contain her joy. With her fingertips she touched the image before the spell was broken and the likeness of her sister faded from the surface of the dark water.

"I've seen everything," said Thildin. "Olara is alive in the city of Klaerthelke."

Riedl came to her then and the women embraced. The weeks of Thildin's anxiety were finally at an end, for now she could be certain that both her sisters were safe and alive.

But Thildin did not tell Riedl what else she had seen, that Olara had a helpmate, and that she was trying to discover a way to set Thildin free.

Chapter 8

In the weeks following Baeul, the king's palace made ready for the arrival of the new ambassadors. Etain's pregnancy was now beginning to show, but still she had not broached the subject with King Lasher. Never the less, she knew it was time to tell him, for it was inevitable that he would know. One day they were sitting together, as they were wont to do, the king half naked on his throne, while Etain's attentions kept his prick fat and hard.

"Sire," said Etain, as she sat on the floor in front of him, ever ready to minister to his cock, "there is something I must tell you."

"What is it?" he said, beckoning to her to massage his fat, purplish thing. Etain obeyed, running her fingers up and down the silky belly of his penis.

Well, I...I..." she started to say, but then she paused.

"Well, what?"

"It's very important, what I'm trying to tell you..."

"Then tell me," said the king.

"I...I am with child," said Etain finally.

King Lasher's eyes widened with surprise.

"How long have you known?"

"For three moons, sire."

King Lasher slapped his thighs and stood up from his great golden chair, his prick erect and bobbing against his belly.

"It will be a fine, strapping boy," he said, "and when he is of age, he'll have half my kingdom." He strutted back and forth with his huge erection, chuckling and smiling.

Etain was not so pleased.

"And what if the baby is a girl?" she said. "Would you give a girl-child half your kingdom?"

King Lasher frowned.

"Of course not. She would have a fine dowry, and perhaps her husband would consult her in matters of state," he said. "But no, even Princess Riedl will never be heir to my throne. What are you talking about, woman?" he said angrily.

But Etain did not back down. Quietly she stared at him with a look as stern as his own. The king broke the silence.

"But why should we quarrel?" he said. "The child will certainly be a boy. Come now, for I want to enter into the secret door of love."

Etain decided to keep still. Instead of arguing, she focused on the king's fat, hard prick. Laughing, he made it pop up and down against his muscular belly. Watching it, Etain felt the juices of her pink cunt flowing.

"Down on your hands and knees!" said the king, "I'll take you from behind!"

Etain giggled and did as she was told. Immediately the king came down from his throne, and threw the pleats of her harem skirt over her back, exposing her beautiful, firm buttocks. With one hand he spread the lips of her sex, while he slipped two fingers of his other hand into the folds of her wet cunt. Rhythmically he pumped her, in and out, in and out, until Etain let out a half moan, half giggle, denoting her pleasure and approval of their pass time.

When he felt her juices beginning to flow, King Lasher took hold of his cock, and began to massage himself up and down. In a few moments, his cock had become desirously firm. He stroked himself a few more times, until he saw the first pearlescent drop of his manhood come to the tip of his prick. He smeared this over the surface of his glans, and then he plunged the dull cockhead deep into the opening of Etain's cunt. Etain took it, and the walls of her sex contracted and clung onto his penis, massaging it neatly with fluttering spasms. She let out a groan of pleasure. She rocked back and forth, thrusting her pelvis backward so it drove his sex deeper inside her, until finally she cried out loud and collapsed on her elbows and knees.

But the king had not been satisfied. He lay down on his back and bid her to straddle his hips so she could sink his prick within her, very deep and warm. Etain did just as she was told, supporting herself on her hands. She pushed the mouth of her cunt onto the head of his cock, sliding down until his cock was buried deep inside her. Harder and faster she pumped, her breathe coming in hard gasps, until finally the king cried out and humped his pelvis forward, rocking Etain where she sat upon his cock. Then he gritted his teeth and gripped Etain by the arms; and presently she felt his hot seed spurt against her womb.

"That was magnificent," said the king, as they lay together for a while on the floor. "My cock hungers for you constantly; but our lovemaking will have to endure some short interruptions, for tonight we celebrate the arrival of the new ambassadors. Let's see to the preparations for our guests. Come, I would like you to see our fine kitchen."

With that he stood up, offering his hand to Etain. King Lasher was excited, because now that Etain was with child, he could add other venues to their repertoire. Etain was excited to be visiting a place in the palace that she had never seen.

Hand in hand they walked through the many corridors of the king's palace until they came to the royal kitchen. It was an immense room, and inside many slaves and servants were busy preparing food. Etain looked around her in amazement at the many baskets of vegetables, fruits, and eggs. In the eastern wall four great ovens had been fashioned, and from these the king's baker was taking out huge trays of finished pastries. In the northern wall there was a great pit, where two whole ferl beasts were roasting on spits. There were tall canisters of milk, and loaves of fresh bread and pounds of cheese. The aroma in the room was delicious, and Etain savored it, breathing deeply of its goodness.

"Would you like to try any of the delicacies you see here?" said the king. "I want you to try some. I would value your opinion about the feast. Chef, have you started on the sauce for the roast ferl?" Then he looked at Etain. "It might be too early to sample a taste of everything, but certainly you can taste a bit of soup, and you must have a taste of our own chef's fine desserts."

Etain was amused and pleased that King Lasher valued her opinion so. Although she had enjoyed a sumptuous breakfast of blanched eggs and Bazulian tea, she was more than delighted to taste the redolent soup and mouth-watering pastries the chef had prepared. The soup was spicy, creamy and rich, and the pastries and pies were, to Etain, without equal. How exciting this night would be, with all the palace decked in extreme splendor, and a magnificent feast besides. With excitement Etain began to look forward to the coming evening, eager to try new foods and wines. And the guests, she thought, how interesting it will be to hear the stories of their far off lands. It had already been an exceptional day, for King Lasher had been pleased about her pregnancy, and the gala event was close at hand.

That evening, as the sun of Gwaehr was making its slow descent in the sky, Etain and King Lasher moved about the large banquet hall, supervising the slaves as they checked the long, mahogany tables, to see that each place was set just right. Along with the customary silver spoons and plates of gold, each guest would also have the optional fork and knife. Most of the men would be using their hunting knives to cut their meat, but it was a thoughtful and modern touch for the Gosgovnian king to provide knives for the ladies as well. As they went from place setting to place setting King Lasher muttered under his breath that he hoped the additional knives would not encourage any outbreaks of violence at the dinner table. Etain was much amused by this, and she had to stifle her laughter with a little cough.

At last the final touches had been made. The slaves and servants hurried about, making themselves ready for the arrival of the guests. King Lasher changed Etain's black collar for a collar of gems and gold. Her slaves helped her into a new gown of green velvet and gold satin. They combed out her long, fiery tresses so that they fell upon her shoulders and hung down to her waist in a most becoming manner. It was time to join King Lasher in the great dining hall. There were a pair of immense gilded chairs on a platform at the head of the hall, and there King Lasher sat, waiting for Etain to join him.

"You are so beautiful," he exclaimed, admiring Etain in her new gown. The velvet bodice of the gown was very low cut, trimmed with a bit of crisp lace, and tight enough to press Etain's white breasts into two soft, prominent mounds. Her hair was shiny, reflecting the golden candlelight that flickered from hundreds of scented tapers mounted in sconces on the walls. King Lasher took Etain around the waist as if no one were there to watch them. Brazenly he kissed her, thrusting his tongue into her mouth, and then he patted her prominent belly and beckoned her to sit beside him.

"Of all the fine ladies that will be here tonight, you will be the most beautiful."

Etain blushed and lowered her eyes.

"I am glad that you are pleased, my lord," she said.

Then they sat together quietly, awaiting the arrival of the first couples, and Etain felt nervous like a child of seventeen. She looked out the window and saw the last violet rays of the sun fading from the sky.

"Will they be here soon, my lord?" she asked the king.

"Yes, yes, they will be here soon," he said, and watching him, Etain realized that King Lasher was nervous, too. His empire had grown considerably since this feast was observed last year, and he had assimilated the cultures of many provinces into the life of the royal palace in Gelstohr. Now, in addition to treasure, the king's palace would be imbued with etiquette and fine sensibilities. The slaves and servants would perform their functions silently and unseen, and the cuisine would be the finest in all the known world of Gwaehr. For this he had imported the most skilled artisans of all his conquered lands, that none would ever call him pirate and barbarian; and for this he would greet the ambassadors of the cowed provinces in the palatial halls of his home with a gala celebration that could not be equaled anywhere in its splendor.

At last the appointed hour had come, and the guests began to arrive. The king's butler, black as midnight, met the guests at the door, and handed them off to a dignified host to escort them to their places at the long tables. This butler, Kraal, had been born in the province of Vasquhn. He wore an elegant suit of silver, and Etain could see, even from where she sat, that he immediately made the guests feel at home and put them at ease. Etain looked at King Lasher, and it was plain that he was pleased with the butler Kraal. Soon all the guests were seated, and it was time for dinner to begin.

The king stood up from his gilded chair, and the crowd before him fell silent. Expectantly they waited while he stood before them, his arms raised in the air.

"Welcome, citizens of Gosgovnia!"

Immediately there was applause, and Etain wondered how much of it was genuine.

"We are gathered here tonight to toast the empire of Gosgovnia that has united the great cultures of the planet Gwaehr," he said. "Since the times of my father's father's father this day has been in the making."

There was more applause, and all of the guests got up to their feet.

"I, your king, have brought you here to celebrate the military might of Gosgovnia. I, your king, have brought you here to acknowledge the greatest government the history of Gwaehr has ever known. Look around you, and enjoy the opulence and glory of Gosgovnia. It is all here, everything, and you shall see it and be awed. Raise your glasses and toast to the long life of Lasher the King. Let the merrymaking begin!"

The guests were seated, and King Lasher ushered Etain down from the platform to sit beside him at the head of the first table. All around them people were laughing and talking, and the slaves began to serve the soup, carrying out trays laden with golden bowls that were brought by the dozen. As the king's table was served, Etain suddenly felt starved. She reached for her spoon and savored the rich, spicy soup, while the king ate and made conversation with his new vassals. As Etain listened quietly, she noticed that a very handsome couple was seated next to them, a tall, lanky man not yet in his middle years who had curly blonde hair and brown eyes. With him was a beautiful woman who wore a bejeweled gold collar, much like her own.

"Etain," said the king, "I would like to present you to Kodohr, ambassador of Beltonia. And this is his charming slave, Elana."

Etain admired the beautiful Elana. Her skin was black, and she had masses of long, shiny black hair that hung in ringlets across her shoulders and down her back. Etain and Elana nodded to each other and smiled quietly, while their masters continued to discuss politics over their meal. Beltonia had been a Gosgovnian province for a generation. There had been no strife or insurrections there for years. Therefore the conversation was pleasant and light, and as the second course was brought out and the wine and mead flowed, the two men were more and more affable, and King Lasher's face became flushed with the glow of pride and pleasure.

"Etain," said King Lasher, as a slave filled his flagon of mead to the top once more, "I think we shall have a diversion with the ambassador and his slave after dinner."

Etain looked at Kodohr and Elana, and she saw how Kodohr regarded her with a gaze of appreciation.

"I would be most honored," said Kodohr, "to join you and the lovely Etain in a late night romp."

King Lasher was well pleased with their plans. The main course of roast ferl and vegetables was served, and as Etain ate the tender meat and delicious sauce, she imagined what the ambassador and Elana must be like in bed. Kodohr struck her as a logical, cool tempered man, unlike King Lasher, who was prone to outbursts of emotion. Elana, however, seemed fiery and assertive for a slave. Her master must treat her very kindly, thought Etain, as Elana is certainly not broken of spirit. Only her golden collar denoted she was a slave at all, for her master evidently did not require of her that she carry herself as though cowed.

As they ate their meal Etain and Elana began exchanging wanton glances, looking particularly at each other's breasts, comparing themselves to one another and warming to each other at the same time. Etain felt able to appreciate the attributes of Elana the slave, while at the same time she felt no less beautiful or desirable to her master, King Lasher. King Lasher had never suggested a foursome before, or any manner of sharing; and Etain found the idea enticing. Elana the slave was beautiful. Certainly King Lasher will want to prick her, she thought. Etain wondered if King Lasher would allow her to be cocked by Kodohr the Ambassador, for she found him comely, and the thought of a little change excited her immensely.

Then Etain felt the hand of Elana on her knee. The palm was warm and small, and for a moment it lay there gently, until Elana extended her index finger and started to caress the inside of Etain's thigh, slowly and carefully, tracing a tingling path upwards towards Etain's puff of red hair. Etain felt the lips of her sex begin to moisten as the finger circled and circled, thinking all the while of what it would feel like to have the ambassador's hand on her knee. She would wait for his fingers to reach into her red hair, and then she would part her legs and allow his big, warm fingers to slide deep inside her sex. Between courses Etain and Elana sat like that, while the ambassador and the king kept up their conversation. Etain stole a look at Kodohr, and caught him gazing at her face and hair. He finds me beautiful, she thought, and her heart quickened in her breast, the juices of pleasure starting to seep into her soft red nether hair.

She grew so wet she began to think that King Lasher, seated next to her, must certainly be able to smell her. He loved the smell of her glistening sex, like a pink shell of the ocean.

At last it was time for dessert. The trays of exquisite pastries and pies were carried to the tables by male slaves with gold collars and red trousers. The king filled the goblets of Etain and Elana with more red wine. The king was in his cups. Now Kodohr stared at Etain quite openly, making Etain's sex pulsate with desire. She ate a pastry of wild honey and sweetened cheese, lowering her eyes to avoid Kodohr's stare, but glancing up frequently to the exciting reality that he couldn't take his eyes off her. It felt so good to be desired instead of owned. Kodohr looked at her with large, soft eyes of brown. Etain imagined that his mind was full of culture and fine sensibilities, that he foresaw a world where slavery no longer existed. Etain felt she knew everything about this man, and that he would come to know everything about her, just by the intensity of his gaze.

At last the dinner was ended. Some of the guests were still sitting and talking, but Kodohr gestured to Elana to get up and get ready to leave. King Lasher was rather drunken, and Etain steadied him as he got up from his chair to his feet.

"Sire," she said to him, "it has been a most memorable evening. I'm sure the king's palaqce has made an impression on the world tonight."

King Lasher kissed her on the forehead and smiled.

"How lovely for you to say so," he said.

The king and Etain led Kodohr and Elana to the chamber where they were often wont to sleep together. Only a few candles burned there at this hour, but a hot fire burned brightly in the huge fireplace with its mantle of ebony and brass. With husky laughter the king immediately pulled Elana down on the bed with him, fumbling inside her clothing while he loosened the drawstring of his trousers. Kodohr took Etain by the hand, and they retired into the shadows, finding themselves a place to lie on the soft, thick carpet. Etain could hear the sound of the king's boots dropping as he kicked them off. She saw him part Elana's legs, and heard him moan as he sunk his fat prick into Elana's sex.

But now she and Kodohr were as good as alone. Kodohr held her by the shoulders and kissed her, sliding his tongue into her mouth softly, pulling her up against his chest and enfolding her in a warm embrace. Then he looked into her eyes silently, and it seemed to Etain that his gaze was searching her soul. He kissed her again and then started to undress her, letting her new gown fall to the floor.

"You are so beautiful," said Kodohr, as he gazed upon her body. And Etain wanted to answer him, to tell him just how beautiful he was to her, but she dared say nothing, for fear they would be interrupted by the king. Kodohr undressed himself, and Etain was well pleased with his slender, muscular form. As he let fall his trousers, Etain's eyes fell upon his cock. It was big and fat, and already it stood firm. Etain longed to feel its silky skin with her fingers and stroke its dull head with her tongue. Kodohr sat down on the floor, and pulled her down so that she was sitting next to him.

"Lie down beside me," he said, "so I can look into your wonderful eyes."

Holding her in his arms, he lowered her to the floor.

"Etain," he whispered to her softly, as he searched her face with his large, dark eyes.

"Kodohr," answered Etain, and it felt so good to speak with a lover who did not have to be addressed as "my lord" or "sire".

He started kissing her face, small kisses on her cheeks and forehead, and then he kissed her mouth as before, gently and deeply. He moved his tongue out of her mouth, across her neck and down to her breasts, where he suckled her nipples until they stood up firm and so sensitive. With his tongue he circled around the nipples of both her breasts. Then he ran his tongue down, down over the small mound of her belly until he came to the place inside her thighs.

With his hand he gently opened her legs. He fingered inside the matt of moist hair until he found the opening of her cunt. Slowly he slid his finger inside, circling inside the slick folds of the hole, until Etain rocked her hips with pleasure. Then he parted the lips of her sex and found the bud of pleasure with his tongue, stroking and licking and stroking; but Etain did not want him to make her come until she had the dull head of his penis battering against her womb.

She wrapped her arms around him and pulled him towards her, not daring to make a sound.

"It's all right," whispered Kodohr, "the king has fallen asleep on the bed."

He moved himself over her so she could feel his cock against her. Then he spread his knees and opened her legs, and sunk his cock into her cunt with one smooth thrust. Holding himself on his elbows he kissed her until Etain's mouth was full of his strong, stroking tongue; and all the while he pumped her with his fat cock until Etain's groans of pleasure were muffled by their kiss.

After they had lain for a while quietly holding each other, Etain sat up, a trace of anxiety pulling at her breast.

"Don't worry," said Kodohr, as even in the dark he could read Etain's expression, "He's still asleep. The gods have granted us this time together."

"If he saw us together like this he would surely be sorely jealous," said Etain, "for he truly cares for me, and besides, he is the father of my child that is yet unborn."

Kodohr took his hand and placed it on the slight roundness of Etain's belly.

"You are with child? Now I see why he would let you be taken by another."

He smiled softly and continued.

"I wish it were I who could claim all rights to you, and to your child that is yet to be born," he said.

Etain's mouth dropped open in surprise.

"Don't talk like that, for surely that could be taken as treason."

"It's only between you and I," he said. "Don't worry. I'll hide my desire from the king's eyes."

"I feel so confused," said Etain. "I had adjusted to my strange circumstances. And now with a child…I don't want to jeopardize my good standing with the king."

Kodohr pulled her to him.

"I understand," he said. "I promise I will always respect the stronghold this gives you, but in my heart, you are mine."

Etain returned his embrace. He started kissing her, small kisses on her lips and neck, and Etain felt the aching begin again. Kodohr had just lowered her to the floor when suddenly Etain heard someone stirring on the bed. She looked up, and saw Elana illuminated by the candlelight. By her expression, Etain could see that she felt lost and unsure.

"Sire," said Elana to Kodohr, lowering her eyes in the face of Etain's gaze. She stammered a little, her eyes flickering up to Kodohr's face. "…the king sleeps," she finally said.

Etain sat up, but Kodohr caught her in his arms again, shielding her nakedness from Elana.

"Yes," said Etain, "of course, it is time to take you to your new chambers. Could you get me a gown from the wardrobe?"

Elana did as she was bid, and Etain and Kodohr dressed themselves. Etain opened the door and spoke to the eunuchs who stood guard there.

"Take the ambassador to his room," she said.

Elana slipped into the hallway, but Kodohr lingered one moment more, pressing Etain's hand in his; and breathlessly Etain watched them go down the dark corridor, her heart churning in her breast.

Chapter 9

It was midnight. Etain awoke from a restless sleep haunted by strange dreams. At her side King Lasher slept peacefully, undisturbed. She looked out the window and saw the crescents of the waxing moons high in the sky. This was the time when Etain was wont to make talismans, and her favorite time to scry. The stars twinkled brightly in the blackness. Etain felt her collar and fretted over her lost magic, for Thildin had come to her in a dream.

A cloud drifted across the sky. Etain got out of bed and went to the window. In the dream, Thildin was beckoning her to the sacrifices. Etain gazed at the three moons with excitement, for she was certain Thildin's spirit had succeeded in reaching her own.

To do this, Thildin must be free to do magic! Perhaps if Etain could charm a talisman she could increase her sister's power, which had reached her across space and time. She looked back at the king, who was still sleeping soundly. Now was her chance, but what object could she use? Her eye fell upon a white silk ribbon that lay on the dressing table, a ribbon she was wont to wear in her hair. Quickly she picked it up and went to the window. Without altar or circle, she drew down the power of the waxing moons, then plaited the charmed ribbon into her hair. Now she would keep the talisman on her person to draw Thildin's soul power to her.

But the charm had been made in haste, under circumstances not conducive to magic. What could she do to assure the power of the talisman? She looked at the bed, and at the king who slept so blissfully. Yes, she could use him well, for with the three moons high in the sky, copulation in the ritual way would add power to her spell.

She moved back to the bedside, and quietly removed her embroidered gown. Then, naked, she slipped beneath the satin sheets of burgundy and gold. The king lay on his side, and his breathing was regular and quiet as she moved closer and closer to him.

She slipped her hand over his side, down into the folds between his legs, where she found his penis, soft and small. Then she fingered and teased until she felt his sex begin to engorge, and the king began to stir. He rolled onto his back, still half asleep, and Etain kept working with her hands, stroking his belly and his cock, concentrating all the while on the spell she was working, while the folds of her cunt grew moist and hot, anticipating the dull head of his fat thing.

The king awoke and threw the coverlet off the bed. He pulled Etain to him, pressing her breasts between his hands, taking the pink nipples into his mouth to suck. His hands ran over her white skin, down her back and onto her bottom, and then with his fingers he poked into her wet love cleft, pinching and pulling at the soft red puff of her hair.

Etain pushed her silken tongue into his mouth hungrily, probing and thrusting, all the while reciting the incantations in her mind. The king's fingers were busy in her love cleft. He wet his thumb with her juices, and then he found her brown hole, pressing and circling until the hole opened, and he slid in his thumb.

But Etain would not let him make her come in this manner, for she required the superior position in order to work her magic. Still kissing him and rubbing on his cock she mounted him and guided the head of his prick to the opening of her sex. Then she pushed her hips down and sank the king's hard cock deep inside her, making him groan out loud with pleasure. Rhythmically she thrust her pelvis while she straddled the king, massaging his erect penis with the wet walls of her sex.

She did this slowly and carefully, making King Lasher feel every stroke of her cunt. King Lasher smiled with pleasure as she worked him, and all the while she was saying the old incantations to herself, building the power of her spell as she brought them nearer and nearer to ecstasy. They didn't speak. Deep inside her she felt the aching beginning. It spread downwards into the lips of her cunt, then into the insides of her thighs. She saw the king close his eyes and felt the first thrusts of his hips as he moved his cock to meet her. She saw that he was very near to coming, so she concentrated on the delicious sensations of her own body, preparing herself for climax. Then suddenly it hit her, and she heard herself calling out as the convulsions of pleasure rippled through her. A moment later the king came, crying out in kind, and the talisman was charmed with the flow of seed and the juices of the womb.

Like fire, thought Etain, as she rested next to the sleeping king. To channel this power we lit bonfires on Baeul and Ultaine, and on Midsummer Night's Eve. She looked out the window and still the three moons of the Triple Goddess floated high in the sky.

As she lay there she ran her hands over her belly, feeling the mound that was beginning to form as her womb enlarged with the child she was carrying. Thildin was trying to reach her. Perhaps this child would be born in freedom, and she and Kodohr would be able to be together. What kind of impossible dreams are you dreaming? she thought to herself, as she stared out of the window into the night sky. She felt for the ribbon plaited into her hair, fingering it while she wished her hopeless wishes. Surely I will wear a collar all the rest of my life, she thought, and Kodohr and I will only have stolen moments together at the king's whim. She thought of Kodohr's hard cock and warm, loving embrace, and suddenly the sadness of her situation overwhelmed her; but the child, she thought, the child will certainly be treated fondly by King Lasher. As she fingered the ribbon in her hair, she resolved again to concentrate on Thildin, and to accept what was for the time at hand.

Chapter 10

The weeks after the arrival of Ambassador Kodohr and Elana passed by Etain as a blur. King Lasher invited Kodohr and Elana to the private bedchambers often. Sometimes he would call them in the middle of the night, obsessed with cocking the beautiful slave Elana. They would have foursomes that lasted hours, with the king and Kodohr making many penetrations into the cunts of Elana and Etain, poking them rhythmically with the fat, dull heads of their cocks. When Etain had Kodohr, she felt filled with love and passion. When she had the king, she could only think of Kodohr's adoring arms and his hard, ready cock. What could she do? She loved Kodohr, and only felt affection for the king. During their romps she masked her passion, and in Kodohr's absence she was careful to conceal her longing for him.

Elana, at the same time, seemed especially inflamed by their foursomes. She never failed to convulse with pleasure when King Lasher pricked her, and frequently she made love to Etain, licking and probing Etain's sex with her fingers. This was done so expertly that Etain wondered if Elana had ever lived in a harem. Elana seemed to be just as hot with Etain as she was with Kodohr or the king. Surely she does not love Kodohr, thought Etain, as Elana did not show any great preference for her master over other parties in their play.

It often happened that King Lasher fell asleep after their rigorous pastimes, especially if he had called for a romp late at night, or if he was in his cups before the play began. Etain was therefore frequently left to bid their guests good-bye, or to whisper with Kodohr alone in the dark.

One morning after they had had a particularly amorous romp, King

Lasher slept late. Finally, when he awoke, he immediately asked about
breakfast. He summoned his slaves and told them that he and Etain would
be breakfasting in the garden.

"Did you keep our guests entertained after I fell asleep?" he said.

"Yes, my lord, they were quite entertained."

"Good," said the king, "for I was thinking of asking them to
breakfast."

Etain felt her heart do a little skip as she heard his words.

"Yes, my lord, that would be quite lovely."

"Go to the ambassador," the king said to his slave, "and tell him we
would be pleased to have him and his lovely slave join us for breakfast in the
royal garden."

Silently the slave went to do the king's bidding. Etain felt flushed and
excited at the thought of seeing Kodohr again so soon. She could feel her
heart beating as she looked in the wardrobe to decide what to wear. She
wanted to make herself as beautiful as possible, while at the same time she
feared her excitement might show.

"Was the ambassador well pleased with you last night?" said the king.

Etain lowered her eyes and blushed.

"Yes, my lord," she said, "I believe he was well pleased."

"Good, for I still find his slave enticing."

Etain felt her cheeks flush hotly. Did he not notice the quavering of
her voice when she spoke of Kodohr? Did he not see her excitement each
time he sent his slaves for him? She was overjoyed that Kodohr would be
joining them so soon, for every day that she was away from him was as
agony to her. Etain looked away from the king as she dressed herself in a
gown of white linen, feeling every heartbeat bring her closer to seeing
Kodohr again.

At last they were in the garden, the table before them laden with
delicacies, and Etain saw Kodohr and Elana approaching them from the
fountain in the middle of the green. When they arrived at the table, Kodohr
bowed to the king.

"Good morning, my liege," he said.

Etain looked at Kodohr full in the face, but Kodohr kept his eyes
from meeting hers.

"And how is your lovely slave this morning?" said the king.

Elana's eyes were averted but she smiled, a knowing, worldly smile. Kodohr answered for her.

"I believe she is right well, my liege," he said, "and I believe she was very pleased to hear that we had been invited to join you here this morning. Elana is very fond of these romps with the king."

King Lasher was pleased. He looked at Elana from across the table. Etain could see that he could hardly wait to prick her again.

The four of them sat down to breakfast. As they ate Etain could feel Kodohr's eyes upon her. Likewise, King Lasher was looking at Elana. Etain wondered if perhaps the king would decide to stage their romp in the garden. It was a great custom in Gosgovnia to have cock and cunt come together out of doors. Etain didn't mind, for she loved the gardens and welcomed the chance to be in the sunshine. It was a private affair. Only the eunuchs and servants that came and went reminded her of the public cocking she had endured before all of Gelstohr on Baeul Day.

Sometimes Etain thought of that day, thought of the long, black leather paddles and the harem skirts that opened in just the right places. Sometimes she thought of the king cocking her aching cunt, but sometimes she thought of Kodohr, taking her there on the wide, wooden stage in front of the cheering Gelstohr crowd. His prick would be long and hard as he pricked her. As he took her brown flower, he would fuck her with his thumb in her pink flower, rubbing her bud of pleasure with the extra fingers of his hand.

Etain could become lost in pleasurable daydreams like that, waiting for King Lasher to announce that he would be pricking Elana the slave; but never did Etain forget who her rightful master was, or how much her love for Kodohr might inflame the king.

The king had finished eating. The slave that attended him poured him a cup of strong tea. Always the king was looking at Elana, until Etain nearly blushed watching them. Yes, King Lasher had developed quite a taste for Elana.

"Come here," the king said to Elana as she was finishing the last of her pastry and tea. "Come here and sit on my knee."

Elana did as she was bid. The king positioned her on his knee just so.

He lifted the hem of her gown, parting her legs and showing the shiny black hair of her sex as he did so. He pulled down the neckline of Elana's gown, exposing the soft, round mounds of her breasts. Elana's nipples were hard and dark, and her black skin was glossy in the sunlight.

King Lasher held her on his knee with one arm, while with the index finger of his other hand he started to explore between Elana's nether lips. First he parted the hair, and then he slid his finger in and out of the partially hidden sex. Then with two fingers he retracted the lips of the sex, so that the shell-pink folds beneath the black lips were in plain view for all to see.

The king kept working Elana's cunt like that, sliding his fat index finger in and out of her sex. Then he went to her breasts. With his tongue he circled around her black nipples, and then very gently he started to suckle them. He sat there with her like that for some minutes, while Etain and Kodohr looked on.

Now Kodohr got up from his seat and came over to Etain. With a silent smile he took her by the hands, and she stood up and went to his embrace. Then he kissed her, a soft, silken kiss that made Etain tremble with joy. Had it been just last night that they had been together like this? Had it been just yesterday that she had felt this fire? They kissed and kissed, unable to pull themselves away from each other. It seemed each time they came together, their foreplay and lovemaking became more heated.

"Let's play naked today," said the king. He stood up and began taking off his boots and trousers. Likewise, Kodohr pulled his shirt off over his head. In a minute or two, the two men stood naked as babes, their hard penises standing erect against their bellies. Etain admired Kodohr's tall, lanky frame and the short, curly hair on his chest. It ran down in a line until it reached the thick, light brown hair that surrounded his sex.

But Etain and Elana were both still clothed.

"Etain," said the king, laughing, "hurry. Our guests are waiting."

Etain slipped out of her linen shift and stood naked before all. Likewise the king undressed Elana, who seemed more than ready to slip out of her clothes.

Then they wandered out into the garden, the sunshine bathing their faces and limbs, Elana and the king hand and hand, and Etain and Kodohr hand in hand behind them.

Presently they came to the fountain, which was surrounded by blue and green hassa grass with their tendrils of pink and white flowers in full bloom. There the two couples lay down on the grass, and the play began.

First King Lasher kneeled next to Elana's supine form and parted her knees.

"This morning I shall taste the Gate of Life," he said.

Kodohr soon joined him, lowering Etain into the grass and kissing her belly until he reached her puff of red hair. Then gently he opened her legs, so that the pink sex could be seen between the lips covered with curly red hair. Slowly he ran his finger from the middle of her sex up to Etain's bud of pleasure, moistening the bud with the deep juices of her cunt. Then he spread her cunt lips to expose the whole sex to his stroking, licking tongue. Etain could feel his face between her thighs as he licked her with his tongue and probed her sex with two fingers of his hand. She felt a soft melting sensation that spread over her entire sex, and the delicious pumping Kodohr's loving fingers were giving her. Soon she was rocking her hips and uttering little moans of pleasure. The melting, stroking feeling made her cunt ache for the fingers, and she felt her limbs softening while her pelvis rocked forward to meet Kodohr's loving tongue. Harder and harder she rocked while the melting feeling spread over her body in waves. Finally she felt her sex burst with juices, and then it was all Kodohr's face against hers, his warm breath and his deep, hungry kisses, his slinking tongue like satin in her mouth, his whispered affections in her ear.

And then Etain felt perfect stillness. Kodohr lay on the grass beside her and held her and spoke softly to her so that no one else could hear.

"Etain, Etain, Etain," he said, and Etain answered him with a kiss, deep enough and long enough to bring some of that perfect stillness to his heart too.

But then his hard cock needed to spill its seed. Again he slid his finger into her wet sex, and again he gently pumped the walls of Etain's cunt, now filled with the juices of desire. Then he covered her body with his and opened her knees with his thighs, and thrust his prick deep inside her, pushing gently against her womb. Deeply he thrust over and over, his cock hardening and engorging more and more, until finally Etain felt the muscles of his arms tighten, and he groaned with pleasure as he spent himself deep inside her sex.

His moans continued as he kissed her.

"I love you," he said.

"I love you," whispered Etain ever so softly, so that none but he would hear; but what good would it ever do them? It seemed fate had allowed them only this, that they should for a time snatch a little perfect happiness from the hands of the gods. Sometimes when Etain thought of the future, she felt saddened by the uncertainty of life in Gosgovnia.

But now, for the moment, she was with Kodohr, and she would not let doubt shadow their joy in one another. Even if we have only this, Etain prayed to the Goddess, please let me be thankful and cheerful in his presence, so that every day we have together will become a wonderful memory.

Chapter 11

It was a warm, sunny day. The town square of Klaerthelke was bustling with activity as throngs of people came to shop from the merchants' carts and enjoy a morning in the sun. It was planting time, and the local farmers had all come down from their terraced fields to buy equipment and seed. The market of Klaerthelke had everything they would need to tend their crops of grapes and their orchards of pears and apples. The vendors of the farming implements were adding their voices to the cacophony of the market place, calling people to buy their trowels and hoes and ploughs, lacquered smartly in hues of shiny black and deep blue. There were foreigners, too, mountain men who had traveled all the way from the forested peaks of the Ahlquinetons, bringing their plush pelts of wild kohn over a hundred miles south to sell to choosey Thelkin furriers. The mountain men had untrimmed beards and wore boots and clothing of black menka hide. They sat cross-legged with their pelts spread out before them, and they stood out remarkably among the brightly clothed dwellers of Klaerthelke, like Juban priests meditating in prayer. The jugglers, clowns, and musicians were doing well on this fine spring day, drawing audiences who stood in large circles around them, throwing them their copper coins. Children screamed and laughed and begged sweets from their mothers, who had come into the square to buy baked goods and butter. The sun had brought the tumult of life cascading into the city, and everywhere it sounded, like the roaring of the mountain waterfalls released from their prisons of ice.

In the midst of the hub-bub were Olara and Gol. Gol was selling his meat pies and homemade sausage, and Olara was with him, happy to be by his side. She watched the milling people come and go, and the colors of their clothing nearly sparkled in the clear sunshine. Everywhere she looked she saw bright patches of red, green, yellow, blue, tumbling in a whirl of hues like brilliant bits of glass. Compared to this, her life in the convent of Brida had been staid and dull. She knew that for her sisters this had not been so; for they were truly gifted by the Goddess, and for them each day in Her service was greater than the last. But as Olara stood watching the busy Thelkins, she knew a sense of joy and purpose she had never felt before.

And then there was Gol.

Her love for him was now a normal part of the fabric of her life, and their passion for each other grew with each passing day. Sometimes, when his mother was asleep, they would slip out of the cottage and find a quiet place to make love in the moonlight. Gol knew all the places where the grass was long and soft. There he would lay her down, parting her legs to lick and finger her sex until she begged for penetration; and night after night this went on, his engorged cock keeping her a content and satisfied woman.

Quietly she stood in the square, watching him with his customers. With every one of them he was cheerful and courteous, whether they be richly or poorly clad. Just standing near him excited her, and while she imagined what pleasure their next night together might bring her, she had trouble thinking about homemade sausage and meat pies.

But Olara did apply herself, both with the merchandise and customers and in their humble home. There were many days when she did not go to town with Gol at all, but instead stayed home with Glendin, to keep her company and help with the household chores. Glendin taught her many skills that, because of her high station, she had never been required to learn in the convent. She helped with the washing and sweeping, and Glendin taught her to bake both white bread and brown. She guided Glendin down the road to the mill, and carried the heavy sacks of flour home on her back to save Gol the trouble after he came home. With Glendin as her teacher, Olara showed an interest in all the details of day-to-day life, and she worked hard to please Gol and her new mother-in-law.

"Could you help this gentleman with the sausage and fish he has selected," said Gol, interrupting her reverie, "and tie them into a parcel he can put into his rucksack?"

"Yes, Sir," Olara said to the customer. "right away."

As the man pointed with his finger, Olara picked up each sausage, packing them all neatly into a stack which she wrapped with a piece of homespun cloth. Then she did the same with the fish, and placed the parcels carefully into the rucksack so the delicacies would not be broken and spoiled on the way home. When the man was gone, Gol pulled her to his side, fingering her nipples that showed through the new red dress Glendin had helped her sew.

"And what now," he said. "Shall we finish early and stop in the glen before we go home?"

Olara threw her slender arms about his neck, for the only answer she could give him was a kiss. Deftly she probed with her tongue, and in reply his tongue reached hers, circling and darting, until Olara felt her sex grow wet with pleasure.

Ah-ah," said Gol with a smile, feeling the passion rise in her. "We'll have to wait until we find a suitable place. Please don't try and take me here in the middle of the square!"

Laughing, Olara thrust herself against his body, and through his trousers she could feel his penis hardening. With one hand she grasped him and began massaging up and down, up and down.

"Then take me to the woods," she said, "I can see you are my slave, and I alone will command you to enter the secret places of love."

They kissed again, and embraced; and then eagerly they set to packing up the wagon for their ride up the hillside.

Night was falling. As Gol drove the gnoba up the mountainside, Olara could see the three moons of Gwaehr rising on the eastern horizon. The sight of the full moons made her think of her sisters, imprisoned somewhere in the land of Gosgovnia. In all the days she had accompanied Gol into town, she had never seen the aliens come to buy. Surely, she thought, they must come back again, and she offered a prayer to the Moon Goddesses to keep her sisters safe, wherever they were.

"Whoa," called Gol, as he drew up on the reins, and the gnoba pulled off the path and stopped. All around them Olara could here the chirping of insects and the hooting of the black manderal. Gol climbed down from the wagon seat first and held his arms out for Olara to join him.

"Come," he said, taking her by the hand. "There's a beautiful grove of lindl trees here. We can lie there and have a fine cocking, and no one will know what we do."

Gol's words made Olara's love cleft moisten and ripen with desire. They left the gnoba to graze peacefully, while hand in hand they entered the forest. Gol led the way. Soon they were standing within a grove of tall trees. The moonlight filtered down to them through the high branches, and everywhere there was the scent of the fragrant white lindl blossoms.

"And now you will be mine!" said Olara, laughing.

She stood on her tiptoes and threw her arms around his neck. He lifted her in his arms and kissed her, and with his large hands he fondled her breasts through the new red dress. With his mouth still on hers, he found her nipples with his fingers. He rubbed and pulled and pinched until Olara felt her wet cunt aching with desire. She untied the drawstring of his trousers, and slipped her fingers in to find his penis fat and hard. She ran her fingers up and down its warm, silky belly, stroking and fondling, their tongues still entwined in a hard, passionate kiss.

Finally the kiss ended and he laid her on the ground.

"Open your legs," he said, as he stroked her cheek with his long white fingers, "so I can taste the Gate of Life."

He pushed the red gown up over her breasts, uncovering her nipples. His big hands caressed her arms and her flat white belly, moving lower and lower, until at last they were in the red nether hair. His fingers parted the lips of her sex, exposing the glistening pink cunt folds hidden beneath them. Gently he licked with his tongue, then harder, massaging the crevice of the pink hole until it fluttered. Harder and harder he worked her, probing her sex with his strong tongue, until Olara rocked her hips with pleasure. She thrust her pelvis forward, aching for the darting and licking, pressing her bud of pleasure against his stroking tongue; until finally the aching burst into a gush of pleasure, wracking her body from top to toe.

"I love you," she whispered.

"I love you, too, said Gol.

He kissed her then, very slowly and deeply, while he ran his fingers through her hair. Olara could feel the dull head of his penis bouncing on her belly. With one hand he reached down and opened her legs. Then, with a single thrust, he plunged his fat cock deep inside her.

He moaned with pleasure when he entered her. For a moment he hesitated, his body softening, his legs parting ever so slightly, savoring the first taste of desire satisfied. Only his hard sex, embedded deep in the wet cunt folds, remained as a dull battering ram; but again the craving surged through him, stirring his blood and sending it shooting through his veins like fire. He pumped and plunged and drove, feeling the cunt folds tightening, battering the womb of the Goddess, until both of them pitched and writhed beneath the eyes of the Mother Moons.

Afterward they lay together like two spoons, Gol cradling Olara next to his breast. For a while they were quite still, but then they played, tickling each other and laughing, whispering words of love to each other in the dark. For both of them the aftermath of their lovemaking was always like this, a state of pure marital bliss; and with each act of physical consummation, their bond of love was strengthened anew.

But tonight Olara had another question on her mind, a question she had delayed sharing with Gol out of uncertainty. She sat up and pulled her shift down, desiring to open the subject with him before they headed home.

"I have a question," she said.

"Yes?"

"On the day I first met you, you fed me with a meat pie and sausage," she said.

"Yes?"

"And I stayed by the cart all day, until the sun was going down."

"Go on, what is it you would like to know?"

"Well, late in the afternoon, two aliens came to the cart to buy, and you seemed to know them."

Gol frowned for a moment.

"A lot of the aliens come into Klaerthelke to shop for goods, and I have sold to many of them," he said. "I don't know them all."

"No, I'm certain you know the two I'm talking about," said Olara.

Gol thought for a moment.

"I really don't remember very well, but perhaps you mean the commander and his friend," he said.

"The commander? You know the commander of the aliens?"

"Yes, I know him," said Gol. "His name is Jason, and his friend is called Younger. They both speak E'Hrglaendi passably well."

Olara's heart was pounding in her breast.

"Does this Jason have the power to launch the alien ships?" she said.

"No, he is just stationed here, with the rest of them. They are governed by a great council of their own people. That's the body that decides where the ships will go."

Olara frowned. For a moment she was silent, then she continued.

"Well, what about their weapons? In E'Hrglaend we always heard that their weapons were more powerful than any known to Gwaehr. They are so small that it's hard to believe. But tell me, is it true?"

"Well, yes, I suppose it is, but they don't kill, they only stun. Why are you asking me all these questions?"

Olara hesitated and looked down at her feet. With her head bowed, she went on.

"I was hoping I could speak with them and somehow convince them to go to Gosgovnia and set my sisters free," she said. She could hear her voice cracking, and suddenly she had to blink back the tears.

Gol took her in his arms and held her.

"I'm so sorry, but the aliens cannot help you. They are strictly forbidden to take up arms against the people of the planet, or to interfere with life here in any other way," he said.

"Then Thildin and Etain are lost forever!" she said. She could no longer hold back the tears. Sobbing, she wrapped her arms around Gol's neck and pressed herself against his breast.

"Please, please, I must speak to them, even if it comes to nothing!" she cried. "Please tell me you will let me meet them, and promise me that if I can get them to do it, you'll stand by me."

"Shh, shh," said Gol, stroking her hair and holding her in his arms. He wanted only to comfort her. "Yes, of course you can meet them, and of course I'll always be by your side."

"All right," she said. "Perhaps they'll be back tomorrow, and I'll be able to speak with them soon."

She wiped her puffy eyes with her hands, straightening her shift as she spoke.

"We have to go now," said Gol. "Mother will be waiting for us."

Olara nodded, and together they walked back to the cart. The faithful gnoba raised his head from the grass when he heard their footsteps coming.

On the way home Olara slept, her head resting on Gol's shoulder; but Gol was immersed in serious thought. How could Olara possibly succeed with her quest? Surely she would not be able to convince the aliens to help her; but in his mind, a nagging doubt lingered. Although he wished with all his heart that Olara might see her beloved sisters once more, he was afraid to imagine the consequences that might bring. He resolved to tell no one of their plan, for surely the people of Klaerthelke would turn against Olara if they thought she would incur the wrath of the Gosgovnians against them.

Chapter 12

It was morning. At the base camp of the Nu Omega 7 operation, human life forms were already beginning to stir. In the east the rays of Nu Omega Centauri, the sun of the Nu Omega star system, glowed red-gold, staining the clouds with shades of crimson and violet, and the spires of the two ranger ships were silhouetted against the sky.

It was an operation spearheaded by the Coalition Corporation, a company that specialized in procuring, packaging, and transporting needed substances to planets that maintained artificial atmospheres in order for their populace to survive. The corporation's home base planet, Alpha Theta 5, was such a world, and had been since a meteor hit it five hundred years before, filling the natural atmosphere with so much debris that no sunlight could penetrate to the planet's surface. But the races of Alpha Theta 5 had been prepared. They had seen the trajectory of the meteor before the catastrophic collision, and they went underground with as many of their planet's life forms as they would need to sustain them.

Nu Omega 7, or Gwaehr as it was known to the planet's native inhabitants, was the seventh planet from the sun in the Nu Omega Centauri star system. Its abundant natural resources had attracted the attentions of older worlds, worlds depleted by over population, pollution, and extinction level events occurring within their planets' atmospheres. A few worlds from neighboring star systems, or even from several space sectors away, had approached the Coalition Corporation to solve their problems of insufficient water, plant life, or trace minerals. For one operation in particular the corporation had chosen Gwaehr. They chose their site and made financial arrangements with their immediate neighbors, the city-state Klaerthelke. This was their modus operandi wherever they went. In this way they successfully avoided hostilities.

But the Coalition Corporation was always governed by the edict of the Council of the United Star Systems, which prohibited exhaustive exploitation of resources and interference in the affairs of the native populations. It was clear that Gwaehr did not have the technology of the Third Intergalactic Era, which more advanced worlds employed to sustain their artificial habitats. Therefore any intervention could potentially upset the balance of power in a world where war was still a problem and races could be competing to develop superior weaponry to use against their neighbors. This rule, which applied to all planets and all ventures where resources were being harvested, had only one exception, and that was in the case of genocide.

The two ranger ships had been built in the finest factory of its kind on Alpha Theta 5. The design of their six neutrino-pulse engines, fueled with gadolinium itryium crystals, was superior to any other patent in Alpha Theta 5's entire space sector. They could bring the speed of the ship into time warp drive within a matter of seconds. The gadolinium itryium also powered the ships' customary barrier shields and wave cannons, which were ever ready to thwart a hostile attack should it be encountered. Inside they were accoutered with all the amenities of home.

Commander Conrad Jason, Operations Chief, was scouting the site with his three best men. Although the operation had never been plagued by disturbances, this was a formality that he had observed every morning for the last five years. The Coalition had chosen wisely in the design of this project, and Jason was more than satisfied with the scheme.

"Did we meet our quota of tonnage yesterday?" he asked Younger, his second in command.

"We exceeded it," Younger said.

"And how about transport," said Jason, "how far behind are we?"

He addressed this question to John Barr, who was in charge of shipping services.

"About a week," said Barr. "I just can't get those damn Hekobians off their asses. It's been a problem ever since we had that big skirmish between the natives."

"Well, if you can't get them to move, find somebody else," said Jason. "We didn't come across three sectors just to dig a fucking hole. How about materials? How are we doing in the mine?"

James Slater, chief geologist, answered.

"We're still going strong on the main vein, and we found two more collaterals yesterday."

"Well, great then," said Jason, "so transport is our biggest problem. Barr, take care of it. Call the Coalition, and get us a deal with the Dalkorians. They'll transport anything anywhere. We can't afford these delays."

With that they finished their rounds. Jason and Younger climbed the rhenium diboride staircase into the main quarters ship and walked to the mess hall to have a cup of coffee. Younger had been with Jason for the full five years of his command. As they walked down the narrow white corridor to the mess hall, Younger began whistling an old Basvfanian tune.

"What are you, some kind of songbird?" said Jason.

"Sure," said Younger with a grin.

They reached the mess hall and stood in line for their coffee.

"Say," said Younger, "do you want to go into town again today?"

Jason shrugged.

"Sure, why not?" he said. "It'll be slow today."

They sat down with their coffee, as they had done every morning for five years. Through the large oval windows of the ship they could see the rest of the Basvfanian sunrise. Jason mused silently, thinking about the two posts he had held before being assigned to the salt mines operation on Gwaehr. It was, at least, a great improvement on his last post on Chi Alpha 6, except there had been plenty of women there. Here he had only the conversation of males to amuse him; but Chi Alpha 6 was cold as a bitch, and when the natives turned hostile, the council of the United Star Systems had made them pull out. And so he had landed here. Although he found it hard as a son-of-a-bitch to deal with a nearly constant hard-on, still, his work was challenging, and the weather was okay. In fact, he had to admit that Gwaehr was a damn beautiful planet.

"Hey," said Younger, "what are you thinking about?"

"I'm thinking about a sharp piece of pussy," said Jason. "What else?"

"Yeah, you got that right," said Younger.

Jason stared out the window, at the breathtaking vista of the verdant Thelkin valley. The wild flowers were in bloom. How strange, he thought, to see plant life growing under the sky. On his home planet, vegetation grew only inside the city compound, protected by the panels of glass and artificial lighting of the herbarium. It sure beats Alpha Theta 5, he mused, or any other artificial world I've ever seen. This place doesn't just have water, it has oceans! And salt, he thought, tons and tons of salt, more than enough to support the lives of the few million humanoids that were born here. Shit, he was lucky to be stationed here for a few years. He wondered what it would be like to grow old here, to be able to call a world like this home.

"Hey, Jason," said Younger. "You're off again."

"Yes, damn it, I know," said Jason. "Come on, let's finish our coffee. I have a hankering for some of Gol's homemade meat pies."

Chapter 13

"Figs! Fish! Fresh blood sausage!"

"Figs! Fish! Fresh blood sausage!

"White bread! Brown bread! Get your fresh baked bread!"

"Sweet dried fruit from Bazul!"

"Sweet dried fruit from Bazul!"

In the square of Klaerthelke, the merchants called out their marketing cries in a cacophony of voices. Olara sat in the wagon, while Gol added his call to the medley.

"Fish! Fish! Sausage and meat pies!"

"Fish! Fish! Sausage and meat pies!"

They had been working all day. Olara ate a pie and a piece of sausage while she sat in the wagon and rested. Gol was tireless, endlessly calling out to the crowd to buy, stopping only to wait on people who came to the cart to shop. Olara looked up at the sun, which was well past its zenith in the sky. Business had been good that day, and Olara was hoping that Gol would soon be ready to go home. And perhaps we can stop in the woods again, she thought, as we did last night. Olara felt her sex fatten as she thought of their pleasurable excursion of the night before.

"Gol, "she said, "we've had a good day. Can we go home soon?"

"Are you tired?" said Gol.

"A little," said Olara.

"Of course we can go soon, especially if you're very tired, but I'd like to stay out for perhaps another hour, if you don't mind. People are buying today. Will you be alright if we stay just a little while longer?"

"Yes, I'll be fine," said Olara.

She finished her snack and climbed down from the wagon seat to help her husband. A customer had purchased some goods, and Olara began wrapping them for him. It was an ordinary day.

She smiled and thanked the man for his purchase as she handed him his package. When he had gone, she slipped her arm around Gol's narrow waist and gave him a little tickle through his tunic. Laughing, he turned to her and kissed her on the top of the head; but suddenly his demeanor changed, and he dropped his hand from her waist.

Olara looked up, curious to see what had distracted Gol. When she did, she felt her heart flip-flop in her breast. The two aliens were approaching Gol's cart, and from across the square, Olara could see them coming.

Instinctively she moved towards Gol, putting her arms around him.

"The commander and his companion, they're coming!" she said.

Gol stood silently, frowning. Again he felt uncertain. Do you realize, Olara, he thought, that if you succeed in enlisting their help, you could be putting all my people into jeopardy? If they help you, how can retaliation be circumvented without destroying the entire Gosgovnian empire? He wanted to speak, but he couldn't, for he had vowed he would stand by her. He looked at Olara's face, full of apprehension and anticipation, and his heart was full of love for her. How could he undermine her in this quest, when the stakes were as life and death to her? He was bound to her now, heart, soul, and body; and if he had to make his vow again, he would still choose loyalty to love over loyalty to his nation.

The aliens were approaching. The die was cast, and fate would soon be set in motion. Now he must leave his destiny in the care of Helkara, the Dark Mother, whose cauldron of blood is the beginning and ending of all things living.

As the aliens approached them, Olara could see that they both carried their small, shiny weapons on their belts. One of them was tall and long-legged, with wheat brown hair that that hung in a forelock over his forehead. He had blue eyes and a wide, easy smile. The other one was shorter and slight of build, with dark brown hair and black eyes. His expression was serious and contemplative. They both wore one-piece garments of shiny, black knit fabric that clung to their muscular bodies and exhibited their nether endowments. The costumes had high, upright collars, with a curious kind of fastening that Olara had never seen before; and, to her great surprise, on the left breast of each there was a five pointed star, stitched in thread of silver, and the emblem of a moon or planet with a ring. They were both fine looking men, and Olara found them a striking pair, at once both different and the same.

As they came up to the cart, Olara found herself smoothing her gown, her heart filled with anxiety.

"Hello," the shorter man said, in heavily accented E'Hrglaendi. "It's a beautiful day we're having, isn't it?"

"Hello," Gol said to the man. "Hello, Captain Younger. I'm happy to see you again. It's been a while, I guess, since you've come to Klaerthelke?"

"Well, we've been terribly busy, but we couldn't stay away any longer. We just had to have some of your delicious meat pies," said Jason. Captain Younger just smiled and nodded. "And who is this?" said Jason, looking at Olara.

Gol smiled broadly and put his arm around Olara's shoulders.

"This is my new wife, Olara," he said.

"Well," said Jason, smiling tentatively. "Congratulations, she's a beauty!"

"Thank you," said Gol. "Yes, she is beautiful, in every way, and a fine wife besides." He kissed her on the cheek tenderly.

Olara looked at Jason, but he had stopped smiling. His expression was serious, and he seemed to be lost in thought. Olara wondered what could be going through his mind.

Younger held his hand out to Gol.

"Congratulations," he said, smiling his wide, natural smile. He shook Gol's hand enthusiastically. "Shall we get ourselves some of these delicious pies? And some sausage, too."

He began pointing with his finger, choosing the fattest, loveliest pies on the cart. Olara picked them up, ready to wrap them; but when should she speak to them about her plan? Now? She felt the color rise to her cheeks as she picked up the pies one by one and stacked them. What should she say? How should she begin? She cut four links of sausage, two for each of them, and she felt her face burn with self-doubt. Soon they would be gone, and she would have missed her chance. With trembling fingers she wrapped the goods in the unbleached homespun cloth. Her opportunity was now, and somehow she must get the courage to take it.

She handed Younger the package, and the men turned to go.

"Sir!" she cried suddenly, and both men looked at her, startled.

"Commander Jason," she said, her voice quavering, "I have to speak to you. Please don't go yet, it's very important."

Jason turned back with a frown.

"What is it?" he said.

"It's something very personal, and I need your help."

He looked at her in amazement. What could this beautiful girl want from him, a perfect stranger?

"Go on," he said.

"You know of the recent war between Gosgovnia and E'Hrglaend, and that it ended with the near annihilation of the E'Hrglaendi people?"

Jason's frown deepened.

"Yes, we heard," he said.

"Well, I am E'Hrglaendi," said Olara. "My father and family, all of my neighbors and friends, were murdered. Only my two sisters survive, but they've been captured and taken as prisoners of war. They've been enslaved by the Gosgovnians! You must help me free them, or the culture of my people will die, exterminated by barbarians!"

"And how do you know they are still alive, if they've been taken from you?" said Jason.

"She has the gift of the Sight," said Gol. "She and her sisters are priestesses of the Goddess."

Jason and Younger looked at each other. It was well known to their people that among the Basvfanians the gift of the Sight was real.

"Please," cried Olara tearfully, "you are my only hope! There is no Basvfanian race that will dare to face the Gosgovnians. Without your help, we are lost!"

Jason looked at the girl with pity. He shook his head.

"I'm sorry, but there is nothing we can do. The regulations of the United Star Systems strictly prohibit any interference in the affairs of colonized planets. We can't help you."

With that, Jason and Younger turned away. Jason could hear Olara weeping behind them as they walked away from the cart. He was greatly moved. When he first laid eyes upon them, Jason could see that she and Gol were a blissfully happy couple, a man and woman who knew true love. The sight of them had stirred something in him, an emptiness hidden deep inside, a yearning he had for something that he didn't quite understand. Jason was forty-two winters old. He had known many women, hungered for them, lusted for them, and had them; but he had never known love. But today he had seen it with his own eyes: the promise of perfect happiness, except for the existence of one hideous flaw, a stain that could blemish all the days of their lives to come.

As he and Younger walked away from the cart, Jason looked at his feet. The desolation that filled him was so complete he could not continue on.

"Younger," he snapped. "Wait up."

Younger stopped in his tracks.

"I'm going back there," said Jason. "We're going to get involved. We're going to take her case before the prelate. This is a clear cut case of genocide."

Chapter 14

Thildin sat in her private chamber, eating a fine breakfast of manderal eggs and bacon. She cut the bright orange yolks with her heavy silver fork and dipped the crispy strips of menka flesh with her fingers. It was a beautiful morning. She sat near a window that looked out upon the king's gardens, in front of a small table of cherry wood that gleamed in the sunlight. When she finished the bacon she picked up a delightful, delicate pastry, prepared by the king's own chefs. Its flaky crust was baked to perfection and layered with wild honey. She looked out the window, enjoying the king's gorgeous flowerbeds while the rich vol-au-vent melted in her mouth. In all her days in E'Hrglaend, she had never tasted such food, and though it was better to be free, she had to admit that life in Gosgovnia had advantages of its own.

The chamber that Riedl had given her was spacious and lovely, decorated and arrayed in a manner suitable for a queen. It had two large windows on its western wall, perfect to catch the warm rays of the afternoon sun, yet hung with heavy drapes of floral brocade to keep the room dark at night. The furniture was all cherry wood; the bed frame with its four high posts, a great wardrobe, a secretary, the table, a chest of drawers, and four chairs. All of these were intricately carved with the head and feet of the wolf, and they were polished to such a glossy sheen that their surfaces reflected images as brightly as any mirror. The high posts of the bed frame were hung with an inner canopy of filmy scarlet silk, and a heavy outer canopy of gold velvet sprinkled with a fine pattern of red flowers. The huge fireplace was fitted with a mantle of hammered brass sculpted with a relief of Gosgovnian warriors battling on either side of the head of the war god Balkohr. Thildin looked around her, admiring the splendor of the room, and poured herself a cup of Bazulian tea.

She finished her meal and got up to sit on the window seat to enjoy the view more fully. There were couples walking in the garden, men of station with their courtesans and wives. Thildin had never been in the garden, for it was forbidden for King Lasher's women to be seen by any male, except for the eunuch-slaves who had been cut and specially prepared for guarding the king's most valued treasure. As she longed for fresh air and the freedom to walk beneath the sun, Thildin thought of Utahr the slave. The empty, shriveled sack that hid behind his limp member was testimony of Gosgovnian cruelty, but his silent loyalty to her and Riedl must someday earn its reward.

She thought of Riedl then, and, savoring remembrances of some of their more heated love play, she began to feel the moist lips of her sex fatten with desire. But it was more than just lust that she felt, for in their daily romps together, Riedl had succeeded in charming Thildin's heart as well as her body. Riedl was an intelligent and willing pupil, and Thildin knew that to Riedl she was like the mother the princess had lost as a tiny child. Every day Thildin felt the love between them grow, and though it was Riedl who always took the role of master in their play, still they shared the same fate as slaves in the land of Gosgovnia.

Today would be another special day for Thildin. Riedl had agreed that they would meet at midnight on this night, in the queen's chamber, where there was a window through which the light of the moons could be seen; and there Thildin would have the chance to draw down the power of the three Moon Goddesses, with the magic of their erotic embrace added to the spell.

From the window Thildin called to the guard to summon her handmaidens.

"Bolgar," she said, "call Illah and Frona for me. It's time to prepare my bath."

The eunuch bowed to her deeply.

"Yes, Your Grace," he said. Then he opened the chamber door and called out loud.

At once the two beautiful slaves appeared, one a brunette and one a pale blonde. Both girls had their hair tied up so that it fell in long tails that hung down to their waists in the back. They were dressed in gowns of sheer muslin, so that their nipples stood up against the thin fabric, and the puffs of their nether hair could be seen below. A pattern of wild berries had been wrought with red thread upon the hems of their translucent gowns. They came up to Thildin and bowed, and the eunuch Bolgar retreated into the corner next to the door. He hid his thick black strap behind him, for he knew that Her Grace would not tolerate a slave to be ill used; and Thildin commanded with natural poise, as the Triple Goddess of the E'Hrglaendi had gifted her to do.

The slave girls went to the wardrobe and took out a dressing gown of violet silk that had been a gift toHer Grace from the Princess Riedl herself. Its sleeves and hem had been brightly embroidered with the green leaves and white blossoms of the magical lindl tree. Thildin disrobed beneath the expressionless eyes of the eunuch Bolgar, and Illah and Frona helped her into the purple gown. Then they accompanied her to her bath, which had been prepared with warm water and sea salt and the fragrant blossoms of hothouse flowers. In the chamber of the bath there was an altar to Hemiyae, the little ocean goddess, who always loved to be near the water. Thildin lit the scented candle of blue that had been placed before her, and then she slipped into the delicious hot water in the great tub of brass; and for a long while Thildin stayed and soaked, attended by her handmaidens, preparing her mind and body for the ritual magic to come.

*   *   *

It was nearly midnight. The waxing crescents of the three moons of Gwaehr rode high in the sky, casting a pale glow into the window of Thildin's chamber. Thildin knelt in the pool of moonlight, consecrating herself to the Triple Moon Goddess of the E'Hrglaendi. The whole day she had meditated, first imbibing the bright hot rays of the masculine sun, and now assimilating the cool pale light of the mother moons, drawing down the power of the union of Kerridorah and her consort, Kernulos the Horned One; for it was the energy of Ultaine that she sought, the pure, burgeoning power of animal lust and carnal desire. To this would all the humors of her body be pledged, and the commingling of the juices of pleasure that would soon be flowing would thus be sanctified.

At last Princess Riedl's slave girls came to summon her. They helped her dress herself in a gown of translucent silver. Then down the dark corridor of tapestries they walked, carrying but three slender tapers to light their way. The images on the tapestries glowed bright as they passed them, falling one by one into the center of a circle of candlelight. Further and further they walked, past the princess's secret chamber, deep into the heart of the queen's palace, where Thildin had never been before. Finally they came to a great door, black as ebony in the candlelight, that had a heavy knocker of burnished brass, wrought in the likeness of Balkohr. Thildin stood between the slaves while the tallest one rapped with the knocker, one, two, three. They stood and waited in the candlelight, and again the slave girl raised the knocker, one, two, three. A moment later the heavy door creaked open, and Utahr ushered Thildin inside, dismissing the slave girls with a wave of his hand.

Inside the queen's chamber was dimly lit with only a few scented tapers. Thildin looked around her at the splendid array, at the gilded mirrors and crystal flowers twinkling in the candlelight. Riedl was there, dressed in a gown of sheer black Harkohnian lace. Her nipples stood out like hard candies. The puff of her nether hair made a delicate mound in the lace below. Her lips were rouged dark red, full and sensuous in the pale white face, high cheekbones tinted rose pink, black eyes lined with kohl pencil and shaded smoky violet blue.

"You have come," she said, moving forward and taking Thildin by the hand.

"Yes, I am here."

They embraced and Riedl kissed her, a deep, slow kiss, their silken tongues interweaving like the branches of a young tree.

"And we have the moonlight, as I promised," said Riedl.

Thildin walked over to the window and looked out at the three moons of Gwaehr. When the candles were extinguished she could see that the room would be bathed in moonlight, especially the great bed, where they would have each other before the working of the spell. On a table next to the window all the items of magic were arrayed, as they had been in the princess's secret room. Thildin was well pleased.

"You've done well," she said. "You've come a long way in following the Path. Continue like this and freedom will be your reward."

Riedl felt uneasy when she heard Thildin's words. Freedom? What could she mean? Surely Thildin was speaking of freedom of the spirit, the trophy of the soul, for it was for this that Riedl had diligently followed Thildin's teachings of the Goddess, to obtain a peace of mind of which none could rob her. Could Thildin have other plans? Her uneasiness persisted, but she quieted herself and said nothing. Then Thildin walked over to Utahr the Slave and took his hands in hers.

"And for you, for you, too, there will be a reward."

Riedl was perplexed. Certainly Thildin was acting very strangely.

"Now come," said Thildin to Riedl. "Let's make ourselves a bed of pleasure. But there will be no tying or whipping. Tonight you and I will be as true lovers."

Then all the disquiet in Riedl's heart was swept away by joy, for never had she believed that she would hear her beloved Thildin speak to her so. In all her days the princess had only known what it was to be served; but now she would learn what it was to love and be loved in return.

Thildin came to her and embraced her, and they kissed each other warmly. Then they disrobed, letting their fine, sheer gowns fall to the floor. A moment later they had thrown back the bedclothes, Utahr standing by with his black bag of instruments. Together they lay on the bed, their arms and legs entwined.

"I love you," said Riedl.

"I love you, too," said Thildin.

Thildin straddled Riedl's face, taking her strong tongue, stroking and probing, into the opening of her pink flower.

"Bring me the fat brown cock," said Thildin to Utahr, gasping with pleasure.

Utahr did as he was bid, pulling the fat glossy cock out of his leather bag. Turning, Thildin parted Riedl's legs and pushed the marble cock piece deep into Riedl's wet, slippery sex. Thildin pumped rhythmically, massaging Riedl's dark pink pleasure bud with her thumb, until Princess Riedl moaned with delight.

Then Riedl entered Thildin's brown hole with her thumb, and probed Thildin's cunt with fingers and tongue, until Thildin cried out with pleasure, shedding the juices of love onto Riedl's eager lips. Thildin fell forward, kissing Riedl's legs, and then upward, finding Riedl's sex with her tongue, licking slowly, tasting the juices that were consecrated to the Goddess, to the magic they were making with their bodies on this night. Finally Riedl's body rocked and writhed, and the bedclothes were wet with the juices of her cunt.

For some time afterward they lay quietly together, savoring the glow of sensual satisfaction, but the midnight hour was near. Thildin got up from the bed and went to the window. Her breasts were high and white in the silvery light, with nipples erect and hard as she walked away. She went to the table and picked up a sprig of sage. Riedl watched her in awe as Thildin began to smudge the room, this queen of a woman who had just been her lover. Thildin's body was magnificent as she walked around the room; her full, high breasts, her narrow waist, her round hips and firm bottom, Riedl admired it all. As she watched Thildin become the priestess on this night, she felt assertiveness emanating from Thildin's person, as if she were suddenly in charge of everything in the room. Thildin sanctified the Four Directions with the incense and salt water, and then kneeled down in the center of the sacred circle, the scrying bowl and lindl blossoms before her.

Riedl watched silently as Thildin gazed into the dark water, and Utahr the Slave stood by, still at his post at the bedside. Thildin bowed her head and murmured the ancient words. Then suddenly she looked up with a gasp, staring out of the window at the three moons so high in the sky.

"It is done," said Thildin, as she stood up, ushering Utahr to fetch her a dressing gown from the queen's wardrobe. Utahr returned with a gorgeous gown of red silk and helped Thildin into it. Thildin saw that Utahr was smiling a smile of happiness.

"What did you see?" asked Riedl, jumping up and going to the wardrobe to fetch her own gown.

"I saw my sister Olara," said Thildin, "and she is putting together a plan to set us free."

Riedl gasped in shock.

"What do you mean?" she said.

"I mean that she has enlisted the help of the aliens," said Thildin. "You have to stand behind me in this cause. It'll mean freedom for us all, and for the known world of Gwaehr as well."

"But how could I play traitor to my father?" said Riedl. "What will become of him?"

"Isn't Etain with child?"

Riedl lowered her eyes and nodded yes. How could Thildin know this, without having been told?

"Then don't worry about him," said Thildin. "He is needed for something."

"But will he be made a slave?"

"Do you mean as he has made a slave of me, and of you?" said Thildin. She shook her head. "The people of the Goddess would never mete out to him what he has meted out to others; but he'll be Etain's, and she will decide his ultimate fate."

Riedl was much concerned.

"But perhaps she feels ill used by him," said Riedl.

Thildin looked at her, a long, hard look.

"Etain will not use him badly. She is a woman," said Thildin.

With that Riedl seemed satisfied, and she asked no more questions. Very excited, Thildin was eager to return to her own chambers. She bid Utahr to call for Riedl's two slave girls. They had waited in the dark corridor of tapestries all this time, so that they might never tell what went on behind closed doors. All three of them were given new tapers to light their way to the other end of the palace.

"Good-night," said Thildin, "and sleep well here in your mother's room. She would have wanted this for you." And with that, Thildin was gone.

*　　　　*　　　　*

Utahr the Slave stood at his post, watching Princess Riedl as she slept. Countless were the nights that he had stood so, for he had been her personal guard since she was a little child. Queen Elga herself had chosen him, when his genital wounds had barely healed. He often thought of Queen Elga as he stood alone in the dark, hour after hour, without so much as the squeak of a mouse or the hooting of the black manderal to give him company. Queen Elga had been beautiful, kind and wise, and when she died, he had missed her sorely. She could never know, he thought, what it meant to a slave boy of sixteen, just to be under her care.

It was just after his sixteenth birthday that he had been taken and made a slave. The war his people had fought with Gosgovnia had been long and bloody, but finally they, like so many nations before them, had been over run and forced to surrender to the brutal Gosgovnian army. He came from a large family, carpenters, simple people, but vicious Gosgovnian warriors had murdered them all. He alone had survived, to be taken to the King's Palace and publicly castrated like an animal; and ever since that day he had been in the queen's palace, and the Princess Riedl had been his only charge.

For a long, long time, he had wondered every day why he had been forced to live, when everything he had ever loved had been destroyed. He hated himself each day, beseeching the gods to give him the strength to rebel and earn the punishment of death; but fear kept him ever obedient, the fear that resides in the flesh of all living things, until finally the sad days of his life became ordinary, and he sought to rebel no more.

And Riedl had always been his special charge. She had been a wonderful child, intelligent and beautiful, the apple of her mother's eye. Queen Elga had entrusted her to him, and Utahr had found some meaning in his existence by trying to lift the cloud that had settled upon the little girl when the queen died. He had been a good and faithful servant; and though Riedl could be temperamental and petulant, still he loved her well.

But now there was Thildin. Utahr smiled in the dark as he thought of her, a thing so rare to cross a stern, sad eunuch's face. Thildin was as splendid a woman as even Queen Elga had been; and now there was the promise of freedom, the freedom to choose love and long life. Now out of choice he would serve the princess and the priestess, and the Great Triple

Goddess that both of them loved so well.

Chapter 15

Spring had passed, and summer had come. The days were long and hot, and, outside the city of Gelstohr, the gentle swells of the hillsides were covered with thick, green grass. Inside the king's palace slaves held long, painted fans to keep their masters cool. The palace chefs made light soups and beverages, and trays of savory sausage and liver spreads, kept the right temperature in great adobe cabinets cooled with running water. In the noon heat the regular workday slowed to a stop, and all members of the palace staff were given an hour to rest. Outside the garden was at its height of beauty. The yellow and orange shaerl lilies grew thickly in rows along the walkways, sweetly fragrant and bursting with color. The lawns, carefully tended and manicured by the gardeners, were plush and green, deliciously cool to the sole of the bare foot. But inside the palace, a long awaited event was taking place. It was happening over the course of hours, slowly and painfully, without any respite as it moved forward to resolution.

*   *   *

"Push, Your Grace, push!"

"Come on, dear, it's almost over."

"But I can't," cried Etain, "I can't. I can't push anymore!"

Surrounded by her slaves and ladies-in-waiting, Etain lay on a great feather bed, laboring in childbirth. For hours she had lain thus, biting on wine soaked linen, crying out for the herbal elixirs which would have alleviated her torture had she been in her own homeland. She screamed out against the misogyny of the Gosgovnian culture as the pains wracked her body in excruciating waves. Would it never be over?

"Push, now, push, the baby is almost here," said the mid-wife.

Etain screamed in agony as the pain gripped her and the mid-wife cried "Push, push, push!"

"The head is out now. Push," the mid-wife said.

Etain gritted her teeth against the linen swath and made one last mighty effort to end her ordeal. And then, suddenly, Etain heard the wailing of an infant, and it was over.

"Look, Your Grace, a fine, beautiful daughter!"

"Oh, she is beautiful. Look at her hair, as red as a copper penny. And her eyes. She has your eyes, Your Grace, like large stars in her pretty little face."

The mid-wife held up the baby, and then placed her on Etain's belly while she attended to the cord. The blood streaked newborn squalled as the mid-wife's assistant helped Etain to sit up.

"Come, m'lady," said the assistant.

The mid-wife placed a tight wooden clamp on the cord and cut it. She handed the baby to her assistant, who took the infant to a bowl of warm water and bathed her. Soon the mid-wife was helping Etain to nurse. Etain was exhausted, but overjoyed.

"A daughter," said Etain. "I knew it would be a daughter!"

"What will you call her, Your Grace?"

"I'm going to call her Brida," said Etain.

"But, madam, what about the king?" said the mid-wife. "Perhaps Sillessa would be more appropriate."

But Etain was hardly listening. She was smiling as the new babe began to suckle her breast.

"Madam?" said the assistant anxiously. "Wouldn't you be pleased to call the babe Sillessa?"

Etain looked up at the women as she cradled the baby in her arms.

"Do you think it would make that much difference to the king if I chose a name for her of my own people?"

The mid-wife's assistant looked down at the floor.

"Please, mum," she said. "Call her Sillessa. That's the Goddess, by all rights. It will go badly for us all here if you don't. It's bad enough that the babe's a girl and not a boy."

While the baby suckled contentedly, Etain looked up and saw that the women were chagrined. For a moment she brooded, but then she thought better of building any anger. She had, after all, the visions of her sisters. Perhaps she and her child would not spend all their days in Gosgovnia.

"And will the king take it so hard," said Etain, "that the child is not a man child? He dotes on Princess Riedl. Surely you are all aware."

"Yes, Your Grace," said the mid-wife. "Yes, you're right. But call the child Sillessa. Don't look for his wrath."

Etain considered, and decided she should take the advice of these country women; but in her heart, she would always know this child as Brida, until freedom should allow her to throw off her collar, and raise her daughter as she saw fit.

"Sillessa," said Etain, smiling. "Sillessa. Light the candles," Etain said to the mid-wife. "Light the candles to the Goddess."

"Good, mum," said the mid-wife. "Sillessa is a fine name for such a pretty little babe."

Etain watched as the candles were lit on the altar to Sillessa that stood in the corner of the room. She thought of Kodohr as she watched them flickering. He was not given to needless wrath. His heart was loving and kind. What would ever become of their love if she were freed? She felt the collar around her throat and looked down at the baby in her arms. Surely the Goddess would be with her, and allow her to raise her daughter in freedom.

But now was not a time for regret or dark thoughts. Somehow, somehow, her life, and the life of her babe, would be under the care of the Goddess. Kodohr, too, would be blessed, and perhaps, by some impossibility, they would be able to live out their lives together in love. Looking down at her sleeping baby, Etain decided that it was with these thoughts she must occupy her mind. Now was a time for perfect happiness, for Brida Sillessa was born.

Chapter 16

Everyone prepared to gather in the great room of the residential ship for the meeting of the prelate and council. Olara and Gol stood in line, awaiting Jason Conrad and the mediator. Then it would be their turn to climb the metal stairs to the inside of the ship. All around them there were citizens of the thirteen free provinces of Basvfania; Nardolians in their long black leather jerkins studded with moonstones and comets of foil, Kordohrians with their blonde beards and long, coiled fingernails. Olara stood and watched them all in awe. Unlike the Thelkins, the E'Hrglaendi had been an isolated people, keeping to themselves, preferring to hunt and cultivate the land rather than trade. Gol had grown up near a cosmopolitan city with a well-established merchant class, but these sights were entirely new for Olara. She stared unabashedly, without a thought that her gaping might cause discomfort or uneasiness to another. Gol watched her and laughed.

"What's the matter?" he said, "Never seen foreigners before?"

Olara smiled and shook her head.

"No, I haven't," she said. "Are you making fun of me?"

"Never," he said. "I just couldn't help but notice the intentness of your gaze. But stare away, if that's what makes you happy."

He smiled at her and kissed her on the cheek.

"Look," he said, "it's nearly our turn to go inside. Are you nervous?"

"More than you can ever know," said Olara. "It seems that life and death ride on what I'm about to do, on the words I choose, and how I say them."

Gol frowned.

"You mustn't blame yourself if you can't convince them," he said. "You're just one young girl, just a single victim of the Gosgovnians. If the aliens decide against you, you must remember you've done all that you can do, and that is more than most could ever have accomplished."

Olara was tight-lipped as she answered.

"Yes, I'm just one victim of the Gosgovnians, and that's exactly what I'll tell the prelate."

She turned her face away from Gol, angry at his lack of confidence in her. Surely the Goddess would come to her aid, and she would speak eloquently to the prelate of her circumstances. Gol looked at her, but said nothing more.

At that moment, Conrad Jason, Younger, and a gaunt middle-aged man came towards them through the crowd. Olara watched them as they walked towards them, especially studying the form of the gaunt stranger, who, she surmised, must be the mediator. He looks seasoned enough, she thought, as she watched them draw nearer. Now she could almost see the features of his face. Above bushy black eyebrows his forehead was furrowed, and he wore a serious expression.

It was Younger, with his long stride, who reached them first, and Olara watched as he put one hand on Gol's shoulder and shook him by the hand. She could hear them talking.

"How are you? How is Olara doing?" said Younger.

"Well, I know she's nervous, and she's starting to get edgy with me," Gol said. "I probably said something I shouldn't have. I hope you can make her feel better. She's upset."

Younger looked over at Olara, and Jason and the stranger joined them. Again Olara could hear them as they started to speak to each other.

"Hello, Gol," said Jason. "This is Blair, the mediator. He's going to get us a good crack at this, he's good."

Blair held out his hand to Gol and Gol shook it.

"Where's Olara?" said Jason.

"She's over there," said Younger, nodding in Olara's direction.

Jason immediately started walking towards Olara. As she saw him coming, it was if a fisted hand gripped her stomach. Suddenly she was unsure of herself, as if the Goddess had forsaken her. She watched as Gol and the other three men made their way to her.

"Hello," said Jason.

He reached out for her hand. Olara gave it to him, but it was limp in his palm. Gol was right. His words had upset her. She searched Jason's face, trying to read his level of confidence. He seemed steady. She could find no sign of anxiety there. But why should he worry, she thought to herself then, he has nothing at stake except his pride. Olara studied him further. Jason is a man of pride, she thought. Perhaps that is big enough stakes for this game.

Next Gol arrived at her side.

"How are you feeling?" he said.

"I'm fine," said Olara, but she averted her eyes to avoid his gaze.

"Just remember," he said, "I'll be with you, no matter what."

"No," said Olara, lifting her chin, "I want to go alone, with Younger and Jason."

"But you can't mean that you want to go in there without me. You can't mean it."

"Yes I do," said Olara.

Jason turned around when he heard them.

"You mean you want Gol to stay here?" Jason said to Olara.

"Yes," she said firmly.

Jason looked up at Gol, who was frowning. He looked hurt. Seeing Gol like that, Olara suddenly felt she needed to give a care about his feelings.

"I'm really sorry," she said, "but if you don't have total confidence in me, I just can't take you in with me. You know I love you, but if I am distracted with insecurity, then my concentration will fail, and my connection to the Goddess will be lost. You must have total confidence, nothing less. I demand it."

For a moment Gol looked at his feet.

"I didn't mean to make you feel I had no confidence in you," he said. "It's just the opposite. I have total confidence in you. Please let me come in. I want to see you be great."

Olara softened to him.

"And you won't be thinking any pessimistic thoughts while you're with me?" she said.

"I promise," said Gol. Then he silently took Olara by the hand. The look he gave her told Olara that he would be kissing her if they were alone. Olara was conscious of her whole body as she remembered her love for Gol. She wasn't trembling now. Instead, she felt strong. How glad she was that their disagreement had passed.

Together they began climbing the metal stairs into the ship. To keep her nerves steady, Olara silently murmured a centuries old prayer to the Goddess, and as she said the words, she felt herself infused with an ancient power.

Inside she found herself in a long white corridor. There were no windows or doors, only cold white walls with blinking consoles. The air was cool and dry. As they followed the line of people down the narrow hallway, she heard a steady humming that seemed to emanate from the ship. What was this place, and what kind of people were the aliens who populated it? She did not know. She only knew that this place was the strangest thing she had ever seen, and, compared to the insides of the alien ship, the foreigners of her own planet seemed common indeed.

At the end of the long white hallway there were double doors. Olara glimpsed what was behind them as two Beulahrkians came out and made their way past her. It was the great chamber where the circuit court of the prelate would meet.

They waited outside the closed double doors. Their case would be next. Behind her Olara could hear Jason and the other men talking, but she wasn't listening to them. She did not know if what she felt was anxiety or impatience. She looked down at herself self-consciously as she waited, inspecting the white shift Glendin had made her and the white sandals of leather that Gol had given her. Suddenly she was terribly unsure of herself. I look like a mere child, she thought. How could she have ever thought that she could go before the prelate to argue her case? She tried to steady herself as a fine trembling began in her fingers. Fervently she murmured her prayers, trying to calm herself.

Finally the door opened, and one of the guards waved at them. Jason and the mediator went in first, followed by Gol. Olara felt the trembling pass over her in waves as she began to walk into the room, every instinct in her body telling her to go back. As she stepped through the doorway, she saw a semicircular box in two rows, each desk housing a member of the council of the prelate. A long white table with many chairs faced them.

"You and Blair and I will sit at the table in front of the bench," said Jason. "Gol will sit behind us in these chairs that are meant for the audience. Are you nervous?"

"Yes, of course I am," Olara whispered.

"Don't worry," said Jason. "Blair is one of the best. Keep your answers simple. Blair will take care of the rest."

Olara nodded, and the three of them sat down. The prelate had been at recess. Now the door opened and she came inside.

"All rise," called out the bailiff.

The councilmen and Olara's company rose as the prelate made her way to the center seat. Olara gazed at her in awe. She was beautiful, tall and slender, with a youthful, womanly body clad in a long black woolen gown. Her skin was dark and her eyes were black and shiny. Her long black hair was braided and coiled beneath a hair net studded with pearls. She wore a long cloak that matched her gown, which had a great diamond shaped clasp of silver that kept the cape draped over her shoulders. As the prelate walked into the room Olara felt the trembling within her lessen. Surely this is a just woman, she thought, wise and strong, who will have the courage to decide this case in favor of the Goddess's people.

"The Supreme Council of Star Sector 9, Star System Nu Omega, is now in session. The venerated Prelate Illykah presiding. All those with business before this court, step forward to be heard. Be seated."

Prelate Illykah struck the desktop in front of her with her gavel.

"Council is now in session," said the prelate. "Bailiff, call the next case."

The bailiff stepped forward.

"Case chi alpha, motion of Conrad Jason and Olara of E'Hrglaend vs. Gosgovnia," said the bailiff.

Prelate Illykah read from a kind of parchment Olara had never seen before.

"I take it you are Blair the mediator and Olara of E'Hrglaend," she said.

Blair stood up.

"Yes, Your Honor," he said. "Olara of E'Hrglaend comes to you today to plead a case of genocide. Her entire nation was wiped out and her two sisters were taken prisoner when Gosgovnia descended upon E'Hrglaend nine months ago. Commander Conrad Jason stands ready to aid her to achieve her sisters' release. They need the permission of the council to proceed."

Prelate Illykah looked at Olara. Olara felt the fine trembling inside her intensify.

"Olara of E'Hrglaend," said the prelate. "Stand before the court."

Olara rose from her seat and Mediator Blair did also.

"What is your complaint against Gosgovnia?" said the prelate.

For a moment Olara stared, searching the prelate's face. The clock on the wall had hands frozen like ice. What should she say? She felt the trembling begin again, stronger this time, emanating deep from within her until it washed over her into the far reaches of her limbs. All the words she had rehearsed for this moment left her as a flurry of thoughts came tumbling through her mind. She knew the seconds were ticking by, but she felt herself frozen in time. Now Prelate Illykah's expression seemed stern and disapproving to her as Olara stared up at the striking woman behind the bench. She felt her mouth go dry as Blair nudged her, commanding her to begin.

"Ten moons ago, after many moons of battle, my people were conquered by Gosgovnia," Olara said. "They were savage and cruel, killing nearly everyone, except for a few miserable captives which they took as slaves. My father, and all my kin-folk and neighbors, were murdered with the rest."

Olara felt the tears coming to her eyes as she spoke. She fought to choke them down.

"My sisters and I lived in the convent of Brida. Etain was high priestess, and Thildin was wonderful at working magic; but the convent, too, was taken. I escaped only because I had been sent out to the village to tend a woman who was sick. Etain and Thildin were taken prisoner, slaves of Gosgovnia."

Olara felt the tears coursing down her face. She lifted her palm to wipe them away, looking down at her sandals as she spoke.

"And we are just a few of the victims of Gosgovnia," she continued. "Gosgovnia has terrorized the entire planet of Gwaehr for twenty years of sieges and bloodshed. It's time their pillaging and murdering be stopped!"

Weeping, Olara collapsed into her chair. She covered her face with her hands, unable to control them, but ashamed of her girlish tears. Had the Goddess forsaken her? How could she have broken down like this, in front of the entire courtroom? Surely her case was now lost, since she had behaved like a frightened, confused young girl.

But Blair was still at her side. Frowning, Prelate Illykah addressed him.

"Mediator, what have you to say about this case?"

Olara watched as the mediator stepped forward to the bench. Prelate Illykah, with her beautiful, light olive skin, sat with her dark brows furrowed on her forehead.

"Your Honor, if it please the court," said Blair, "we find this to be a clear cut case of genocide. Gosgovnia descended aggressively upon the people of E'Hrglaend without provocation. Except for a few survivors, the Gosgovnians did their best to decimate an entire culture. And, as Olara has said, the Gosgovnians have perpetrated this on many peoples of Gwaehr. At the court's discretion, these crimes could be mitigated. Commander Conrad Jason awaits only the permission of this council to go in and save the last of the E'Hrglaendi from slavery."

Prelate Illykah turned her intent gaze upon Olara.

"And how do you know that your sisters Etain and Thildin have survived?"

"I have the gift of the Sight," Olara answered.

"Is this true, mediator?" asked the prelate.

"Yes, and we have verified it," said Blair.

For a moment, the prelate fell silent.

"In deciding this case, we could be setting a dangerous precedent. I am sure it is well known to you all that there is a stringent ordinance against the Coalition intervening in the affairs of native populations."

Olara had dried her tears. Now she sat at full attention, her heart hanging on each word the prelate spoke.

"This council has heard the evidence presented before the court. There will now be a recess while the council considers this evidence and decides the outcome of this case."

Prelate Illykah rapped sharply with her gavel, and then she and the councilmen filed out of the room into the prelate's chamber.

Blair put his hand on Olara's shoulder.

"You spoke very well," he said. "It's a good sign that she took the council back into her chambers. She must be thinking of deciding in our favor, or she would have immediately cited the ordinance. Now we have to wait."

Olara stood up, and she felt as if her body had been drained of energy. How could they possibly win? In a moment, Gol was beside her.

"You were wonderful," he said.

"But I broke down, like a child!" she said.

"But perhaps in this case your tears were as eloquent as any words could ever have been," said Gol.

Conrad Jason now joined them. It seemed like an eternity had passed, but in reality, it had only been a few minutes, and the bailiff came out once more and stood before the courtroom.

"All rise," said the bailiff. "Court is back in session."

Prelate Illykah sat down at her bench and rapped the desktop with her gavel.

"The council has met and considered the evidence presented here today," said the prelate, "and though this has been a difficult decision for us to make, the council has decided in favor of Olara of E'Hrglaend, and deems it appropriate for Commander Jason to aid her in the release of her sisters, Etain and Thildin. Court is adjourned."

Olara's mouth dropped open as the gavel sounded with another crack, and then her face lit up with a smile of gladness that lit her face from ear to ear. Olara looked up at Prelate Illykah, and saw that she was smiling back at her. Could it be true? They had won.

Chapter 17

"All right, Younger, what have we got?"

"The men are ready, sir. "

"Weapons?"

"Just as you specified, sir. Shuttle force fields on level six. Shuttle phasers on level seven. Hand held phasers on high sweep."

"Good," said Conrad Jason. "And the restraining gear?"

"This is the Coalition's largest shuttle, sir," said Younger, "but there is room for only six prisoners."

"That's fine, six is about all we'll need."

"Sir!"

"And what about the restraints themselves?" said Jason.

"Hard leather, Sir," said Younger. "About an inch thick. And that's before we put them into their collars and beam tubes."

Jason was satisfied. At the thought of collaring and shackling the prisoners, he felt his sex begin to grow rigid. He looked at Younger and saw that he already had a hard-on, quite visible beneath his slick uniform. Jason began to chuckle.

"I see you've got one, too," he said to Younger.

"Sir?"

"A hard dick," said Jason.

Younger grinned.

"The next best thing to a pretty pussy," said Younger, "is a skirmish."

"Are we young enough to remember the last time we saw either one?" asked Jason.

"Hardly, sir," said Younger. "I'm working strictly on imagination."

Jason laughed again. He remembered his last good fuck, a bronze skinned black-eyed beauty on Chi Alpha 6; face like a vixen, black hair like satin, breasts like pomegranates. Her dark pink pussy was slick as he rubbed the head of his cock in her juices. He sucked and bit at her hard nipples as she squirmed, her wrists in tight leather cuffs bound firmly to the iron ring in the wall. What was her name? Janet, yes, Janet. Actually, Janet was mostly a dyke. The only thing that had persuaded her was Jason's over-sized cock. He remembered how tight she was when he pushed in his fat thing.

"Oh, yeah? So tell me about your last good fuck," said Jason.

"Sir!"

"Forget the "sir" for a minute, Younger. Last Good Fuck. That's an order."

"Well, sir…I mean … sir … she was an attractive native girl on Epsilon Theta 9," said Younger.

"What color was her hair?"

"She had dark brown hair, sir, and her eyes were green."

"And her breasts, what about her breasts?"

"I don't remember her breasts, sir. It was her cunt that made her such a good fuck. It was like wet velvet. Practically sucked me as I shoved it into her."

Jason sighed.

"Probably be a while until we see that kind of action again," he said. "I guess we'll have to settle for a skirmish for now."

"Yes, sir!"

Jason stared at Younger for a moment. After all, this was his best friend. Battle caused changes.

"What was her name?"

"Layla, sir!"

"Did you tie her up?"

"Yes, indeed, sir, I sure did!" exclaimed Younger.

"Good," said Jason. "Just want to make sure I'm dealing with the right kind of man."

"Yes, sir!"

"Shut up," said Jason.

Younger grinned.

"Permission to board ship, sir!" said Younger.

"Permission granted," said Jason. "What about Gol and Olara?"

"Already aboard, sir!"

"And the maps?"

"Sir, I've seen to everything, sir!"

"Alright then, alright. You're starting to get on my nerves. Get aboard."

Younger started up the shiny black staircase to the shuttle, and Jason followed. Thirty of Jason's best men were awaiting them inside. The shuttle engines hummed like a sine wave, louder then softer, in a rhythm as steady as a heart beat. It was a very large shuttle, and Jason felt his engorged cock pulsing as he arrived into the ship's interior. This would be one of his most exciting ventures ever.

Gol came forward as Jason walked to the head of the bridge.

"Hello," he said.

"Good morning, Gol. How is Olara?"

"Nervous, but excited. This is a big day for her."

"And for us all," said Jason.

Olara smiled at him. She was already buckled into her seat, ready for take off.

"You have the maps, Gol?" said Jason.

"Yes, sir. Younger has taken care of everything. I don't think we'll have any trouble finding our way there."

"Hopefully the rest of the operation will go as smoothly then," said Jason. "Hey, this is a pretty fancy machine. Are you sure you can pilot this thing?"

Younger grinned at Jason from his seat at the bridge.

"Yes, sir!"

"Alright, then." Jason turned and faced his crew of thirty. "Men, you've had your briefing. Remember this is a volunteer mission. We all know this has the potential to be a very dangerous foray; but I want to reiterate the edict of the Council of Star Space Sector 9. Even though our own lives may be in danger, we are prohibited from taking any life ourselves. All weapons will be set, as always, on stun. If any of you fail to follow this order, you will be court marshaled and sent to Beta Nu 11, where you can mine coal and freeze your asses off for the next twenty-five years. Is that clear?"

A chorus of masculine voices rose loudly from the crew of thirty.

"Yes, sir!"

Jason sat down in his seat at the bridge, next to Younger. Gol was directly behind them, with Olara at his side. Jason turned in his seat to address Olara.

"Has the Sight told you more about exactly where your sisters are located?"

"Yes," said Olara. "Last night it came to me in a dream. There are two palaces in Gelstohr. My sister Etain is in the king's palace, held by King Lasher himself. Thildin is in the queen's palace, where the king keeps hundreds of women captive in his harem."

"I guess they'll be glad to see us coming," said Jason.

"Ready for take off," said Younger.

Younger pressed a blinking button on the control panel and the hum of the shuttle engines grew louder. Moments later, they were airborne.

"We're on our way," said Jason, feeling his hard dick plastered against his belly. "We're on our way."

Chapter 18

Their fingers slid in and out of hot, wet cunt folds. Their two pink flowers were as one, throbbing with desire, as they suckled each other's tongues in a long, deep kiss. Riedl found Thildin's nipples and began to rub. Then, back into the nether hair, Riedl's fingers probed eagerly into the succulent pink star that awaited them. Thildin began to rock her pelvis as Riedl pumped and pumped, now with two fingers, grabbing at the slick walls of Thildin's sex as she worked the body of her slave. Thildin's wrists were bound in tight, narrow thongs of leather that bit. Thildin moved to shift her cunt, her sex throbbing with the rubbing of Riedl's caressing thumb. The sheer, shiny gold panels of Thildin's harem skirt had been thrown wide. Now Thildin wrested against the stinging leather bracelets that kept her tethered tight, sliding her wet sex against Riedl's expert fingers. Soon she knew that Riedl would command her to part her legs, and then the licking would begin.

"Slave," said Riedl, "expose your sex!"

Thildin did as she was bid, opening her long legs so that the shell-pink surfaces of her glistening cunt were exposed.

"Bring the whip," said Riedl.

Utahr came to the bedside, drawing the whip of knotted thongs from the black leather bag.

"Whip her!" cried Riedl.

Utahr began the whipping while Thildin moaned, always careful to keep her throbbing sex exposed. She received the customary thirteen strokes.

"The wine," said Riedl.

Utahr picked up a crystal flask. From it he poured dark red wine on Thildin's sex. It made the raw spots sting and burn. Thildin whimpered, raising her head to tempt Riedl with her lips. Riedl stopped what she was doing and kissed her, thrusting her tongue deep into Thildin's mouth; but

Riedl soon took charge again, and turned her attention once more to Thildin's cunt.

Now the licking would begin.

"You've had your punishment," said Riedl. "Now lie still for my tongue."

Riedl began to lick and suck. Carefully she massaged the outer folds of Thildin's cunt with her silken tongue. Then, as Thildin's sex fluttered open, she probed more deeply, tasting Thildin's juices and massaging the flower-like opening. Finally Riedl slid in her thumb eagerly. Thildin moaned and her sex fluttered and opened, fluttered and opened, its juices flowing, while Thildin rocked her sex in satisfaction.

After it was over, they lay side by side and Riedl caressed Thildin's breast with her fingertips. The sunlight bathed them warmly as they lay on the red silken coverlet. Suddenly Riedl had a funny feeling and she wanted desperately to tell Thildin about it.

"I have this sense that something unusual or important is going to happen today. What do you think? Do you have the same feeling too?" said Riedl.

Thildin propped her head up on her elbow.

"Well," she said, "I have to admit I was very pre-occupied by our lovemaking," said Thildin. "No, I haven't sensed anything unusual."

Thildin held her breath and searched Riedl's face with her eyes. Could it be happening? Was her young student finally developing the Sight?

"But I'm sure of it," said Riedl. "Please, couldn't we throw the cards?"

"Of course, and we have to, if the feeling is so strong in you," said Thildin.

Thildin got up from the bedside and went to the table where the magical implements were kept. From a small drawer she drew out a deck of delicately painted Tarot cards. She sat cross-legged on the floor with the cards in her hand.

"Light the incense and draw the circle," Thildin said.

As she had been so carefully instructed to do, Riedl consecrated the four directions with the incense and salt water and then joined Thildin in the center of the sacred space. Thildin handed her the cards.

"Now," said Thildin, "it is you who must shuffle the cards, and you who must lay out the formation of the crossroads. Today you will call upon the wisdom of those who have gone over into the place where the mist meets the sea."

Riedl's hands shook as she shuffled the cards, one, two, three. Then she carefully laid down two cards crossing each other in the center of the spread, with four other cards laid down clockwise, each card corresponding to the four cardinal directions. Then to the right of this spread she laid out four more cards from bottom to top in a vertical bar. This was the emblem of the crossroads, the doorway between the mortal world and the world of the spirits and the dead.

"Now," Thildin commanded, "you are ready. Read."

With trembling fingers, Riedl turned over the crossed card in the center of the spread.

"The Nine of Swords," said Riedl. "Our present position … misery, unhappiness, anxiety over loved ones."

"Go on," said Thildin.

Riedl turned over the next card.

"The Five of Swords, reversed. Possible defeat, or mishap befalling a friend? What do we make of this? Are these the forces that cross us now?"

Thildin frowned, but only nodded for Riedl to continue. Riedl turned over the card that faced the north.

"The Chariot, reversed; to be conquered, overwhelmed, a sudden collapse of plans. This does not bode well for our destiny," said Riedl, but she continued to turn over the cards.

Now she came to the card that faced the east.

"Justice, reversed; it is clear our lives in the past have been dominated by intolerance and abuse," said Riedl.

She turned over the card that faced the south.

"Look, it's the Chariot ! Strong forces have been put into motion by someone or something. They are moving towards us, for better or for ill."

Riedl turned over the card that faced the west.

"The Knight of Wands, reversed; there will be unexpected change and fighting."

Riedl moved to the seventh card at the bottom of the vertical bar.

"And now we see ourselves … Ah, the Page of Coins. The spirits have seen how we apply ourselves to the sacred arts. Perhaps this will stand us in good stead."

Riedl turned over the eighth card.

"The Three of Cups. It shows our influence on the coming forces may be able to bring about solace and healing. Perhaps the spirits are with us."

She came to the ninth card.

"Now we'll see what's truly in our hearts … The Star. We are full of hope, faith, and spiritual love. We blend the past and present within our hearts. Surely the Goddess will be with us."

Then Riedl came to the tenth and final card. She held her breath as she turned it over, the card that more than all the others would tell the final outcome of their destiny.

"It is the Wheel of Fortune," said Riedl. She sighed. "There will either be great gain, or great loss. Our destiny is still so very uncertain."

"Yes," said Thildin, "but you've read well, and you were right. Something is afoot. Riedl, bring the lindl blossoms and the scrying bowl."

Riedl did as she was bid, bringing first the scrying bowl, and then the creamy lindl blossoms. They were dried after their harvest in the spring, but fragrant still. She entered the sacred circle again and knelt beside the scrying bowl, which stood on the floor in front of Thildin. Murmuring the ancient incantation to the Seeing Eye, Riedl sprinkled a circlet of petals around the scrying bowl. Then she crushed the rest and let them fall, floating, on the still, dark water of the crystal bowl.

"Look into the Abyss," said Thildin. "Look into the waters of the spirit world from which all living things are born, and to which all life forms will ultimately return."

Murmuring the sacred words, Riedl concentrated on the surface of the water. The fragments of lindl blossom floated to the rim of the bowl, leaving the center of the dark water still and clear. Their creamy reflections glinted and sparkled upon the limpid pool. Whispering the words to the Goddess, Riedl felt her soul drawn down, down into the primal liquid that was the doorway to the beyond. Now, thought Riedl, now, the spirit world would surely yield up its secrets to her.

And then with a rush it was if her entire being were submerged beneath the surface of a vast, cold, crystalline lake, and above her the sky was black and full of flaming comets that rocketed past her and burst into showers of light and color. The liquid filled her nostrils and weighed upon her chest and she couldn't breath. Terror gripped her as she struggled upward to the sky, but there was no movement, only the icy coldness and strange, deep sounds, emanating towards her from all directions, voices of the dead clamoring to be heard. There was no self here, no sense of the passage of time, but surely somewhere the minutes and seconds of her life were still ticking by, slipping away from her into eternity. Clearly she heard them now, the voices calling her name, calling her back into the chilly black womb where being forever ceases.

But then the tightness in her chest eased, and it was if she were lifted upon a high, warm wind, carried weightlessly into perfect blackness. The voices of the dead receded behind her, and all was still. She breathed deeply and opened her eyes, and before her on the floor was the bowl of fragrant water.

Then the images began to appear. She saw a young girl with long hair like burnished copper, surrounded by men in strange black clothing. They were in a curious vessel that could rise upon the air. They were all intent upon some dangerous goal, and it seemed they were looking for something; but then the images faded, and Riedl was left with a deep sense of foreboding. She drew her breath in sharply.

"They're coming," she said.

"You've seen them? Did you see my sister Olara?"

"Yes, yes, I'm sure I did," said Riedl. "She's coming with many men, in a ship that flies. These must be the aliens I've been told about, and their weapons are supposed to be far superior to the bow and spears. Surely they will be able to set us free. But ..."

"But what?" said Thildin.

"I don't know," said Riedl. "There is something very wrong, something I couldn't see. Oh, I want so much to be free, but I'm afraid. Something terrible is about to happen!"

"How many men were with her?"

"I'm not sure, perhaps twenty or thirty."

"Then they must be planning to rely on their weapons, for they are certainly outnumbered," said Thildin. "And besides, they might have trouble finding us. Even with maps, and Olara's gift of the Sight, we can hardly expect them to know where we are, hidden in this palace. We must find a way to get outside into the garden, or perhaps we could send someone we could trust, someone who could show them the way."

"What about Utahr?" said Riedl.

The faithful eunuch stood silently, as always, at the head of the bed of love, the black leather bag hanging from his shoulder.

"Will you do this for us?" said Thildin. "Do you think you could get into the garden to show them the way? It might be dangerous, but it could mean freedom, freedom for us all."

Utahr took a step forward, and for the first time Thildin saw him smile.

"Yes, Your Grace, I'm sure I could handle it."

"Good," said Thildin. "Now all we need to know is when they will be arriving. Did you see it Riedl? Will they be coming by night or by day?"

"I think by night," said Riedl.

"Then we must be prepared. Riedl, tonight you and I will sleep here in my chamber, and, Utahr, as soon as night falls you must go to the passageway and into the garden if you hear the slightest thing."

"Yes, Your Grace, I can do this. You can rely on me," said Utahr.

"Will you have any trouble with the other guards?" said Thildin.

"I think not," said Utahr. "I can tell anyone who would ask that the princess has sent me on a personal errand, and besides, I know all the hiding places in the palace."

"Good," said Thildin. "Once you meet them, hopefully you will have no trouble bringing them back inside. We will be waiting for you."

She turned to Riedl, who had moved to the window where she stood, solemn and quiet, gazing outside upon the king's gardens. Thildin could guess her thoughts. Would nightfall bring bloodshed into the orderly life she had known? Would her betrayal of her father cost him not only his kingdom, but his life as well? How could she reconcile this selfish act, which could only mean disaster for her people, with the path of the wise woman? And finally, would they escape at all? As she watched her by the window, Thildin could feel the tension in Riedl's body as this battle was waged in her soul. After all, thought Thildin, for Riedl this night's work would mean leaving her homeland, the loss of everything she has ever known. She wanted to approach her, but hesitated. Perhaps Riedl needed to be alone.

But Riedl turned away from the window and faced Thildin of her own accord. Her dark eyes were large and luminous, shining with what Thildin thought might be the beginning of tears. But no, thought Thildin, Riedl was not a woman who cried. For all her fire she was resilient and strong, and as Thildin took in her dispassionate expression and her shining eyes, she knew Riedl had made her decision.

"Are you with us?" said Thildin.

"Yes, I am with you," said Riedl.

"Good," said Thildin. "Then we stand together, and the Goddess will bring us our destiny."

Chapter 19

Night had fallen. The three faces of the Moon Goddess were hidden behind a dense bank of clouds. Utahr padded through the corridors of the palace, making his way silently to the northern entrance of the queen's palace, where he could slip into the passageway and await the coming of the offworlder ship.

He went over his instructions in his mind. First he would lead the offworlders into the king's palace, where the king could be taken prisoner and Etain and her baby could be set free. Then he would return to the queen's palace to rescue Thildin and Princess Riedl. He felt alert and excited. All of his boyhood desires were warm in his breast again. I can do this, he thought to himself, slipping from shadow to shadow. No one stopped to question him. Soon he would reach the passageway and the heavy door with its barred window. There he would be able to see all of the king's gardens. He thought of how he would approach the king's palace, just across the grass and past the courtyard fountain.

Only one more room to cross. He held his breath, searching out the blackest shadows in the room. He darted across the floor, blending in with the darkness against the far wall. Then two strides more, and he had reached the passageway. The hairs on his neck rose as he turned his back on the room he was leaving behind. His breaths were short and rapid as he moved silently down the passageway. He was afraid to look behind him as he reached the garden door. He pressed his palms against the cool, polished surface of the wood. Finally the first step of his mission was behind him. As soon as he had calmed himself he looked out the window onto the gardens. It was black and quiet outside.

He began to plan how he would move across the grass. There were no guards in the gardens, for they were all stationed inside the palaces and outside around the circumference of the great garden wall. They would see the offworlder ship coming, and certainly he would have only a few moments to accomplish his task. I hope the offworlders will be well-prepared for this, he thought, for this is no small thing for a few men, no matter how superior their weapons might be.

Then he was left to wait. He pressed himself up against the wall of the passageway, making himself invisible in the darkness so he wouldn't be caught when the palace guards made their rounds. He heard footsteps coming. It must be midnight, he thought, and they are checking security now. He held his breath as the footsteps came nearer and nearer. The sound stopped, and Utahr knew the guards were standing at the entrance of the passageway. The beating of Utahr's heart marked the passage of time. Did the guards suspect something? He pressed himself even closer to the wall, stifling the sound of his breathing until he heard the footsteps walking away. It would be two hours until they made their rounds again. He slithered back to the window. He couldn't see the positions of the moons in the sky.

How much time had passed, and would the offworlders arrive before he was discovered? He thought of Thildin and Princess Riedl. What would become of them if he did not succeed? Surley they would all be beheaded, and perhaps Etain and her baby would be put to the sword as well. In Gosgovnia the punishment for treason was swift and brutal. Utahr remembered the ambassador Boraal, who had planned an insurrection that failed. His trial had lasted but a day, and within a week he was taken to Gelstohr and publicly disemboweled and beheaded.

The waiting was unbearable. He looked out the window and saw nothing but the peaceful gardens draped in darkness. When would they finally arrive? His legs ached from tension, he didn't know how long he had been hiding. Surely if I am captured here, lurking near the garden door, I will be taken and torured for the truth. He thought of a favorite Gosgovnian torture, which was to skin a man alive. It was almost as horrible as being burned alive.

Suddenly he saw something in the southern sky. It was black and he couldn't make out its shape as it barely broke through the dense layer of clouds. It disappeared again, and he could hear or see nothing. He listened for any sounds of soldiers running through the palace.

And then the great vessel appeared in the sky. It was dull black and diamond shaped with a great dome at its center. The ship hovered a moment outside the wall. A flash of light emanated from its prow, and swiftly it descended, landing near the king's palace on the eastern edge of the green.

Finally, finally they have come! he thought. As Utahr lifted the iron bar that secured the door he listened for footfalls behind him, but still he heard nothing. He opened the door and darted to the trees.

He crouched in the darkness against the great trunk of an old harl tree. A faint humming emanated from the ship. A hatch opened, exposing a staircase that led into the ship's belly. The offworlders came off single-file, their small, shiny weapons in their hands. It's now or never, he thought, and he left his hiding place and ran towards the offworlders, holding his hands in the air to show he came unarmed. As he reached the ship, the man who appeared to be the leader approached him.

"You must be a friend," the man said, but Utahr could not understand his language. He beckoned the man to follow him.

The commander waved to his squadron, and they followed Utahr as he ran to the door that led to the king's palace. At the doorway the commander raised his weapon and vaporized the door.

Utahr ran inside, and he heard the footfalls of the sentries coming. He waved again at the commander and his men to follow, always follow. The long corridors of the palace were dark, but Utahr knew his way well.

They reached their final approach to the king's chamber. They surprised the guards at the door, and the commander felled them with his weapon. Utahr saw them fall, and whether they still lived Utahr could not tell. The commander burst into the room where Lasher and his concubine lay sleeping.

"Etain!" the commander called. The sleeping couple sat bolt upright in the bed. The commander used his weapon, and the king fell back upon the pillows as though lifeless.

"Hurry, Etain," the commander said. "We have come to get you and Thildin."

"But the king!" Etain said.

"Don't worry," the commander said in his thickly accented E'Hrglaendi. "He is still alive. We are taking him with us, he'll make a valuable hostage. Brown, Johnson, get him to the ship. Barr and Stevens, you cover them." He turned to Etain. "Where is Thildin?"

Utahr heard Thildin's name spoken, and he spoke in Gosgovnian to

Etain. "My lady, Thildin is in the queen's palace with Princess Riedl. The princess has also been involved in this plan, and both of them must be set free. I can lead the way."

"But who are you?" Etain said.

"I am Utahr, the princess's slave and body guard. I have been promised freedom too. If you don't take me with you, I will surley be put to death for treason."

Suddenly an infant began to cry. The commander looked around him. "There's a baby?" he said.

"Yes," Etain said.

"God, I hope I can get you all out safely," he said. He turned to his men. "Move it, now!"

Swiftly they ran through dark hallways, the commander and his men always ready with their weapons.

"This way," Utahr called. He let the commander and his men move ahead of him as they entered the passageway back out into the gardens. Brown and Johnson hesitated in the doorway, the limp figure of the king straddled between them.

"They're swarming all over," Brown said as he and Johnson made their way out with the king. "Keep us covered!"

Etain lowered her head, held her baby to her breast and ran out into the open towards the ship. She heard the zing of an arrow pass her head, but still she ran for the open hatch in the ship's belly, reaching its safety just as the Gosgovnian archers regrouped around her. The offworlders' weapons struck them down, but still the arrows sang in the darkness, and Utahr saw three of the commander's men fall.

Utahr shouted to the offworlders as he ran toward the queen's palace. Jason vaporized the door and followed Utahr down the long corridors, deeper into the queen's palace. On either side of the hallway curious women, who now were left unguarded as the king's sentries engaged in battle, came to their doors to investigate the commotion. At every doorway they stood in their long dressing gowns, watching as Utahr and Jason's men passed.

Finally Utahr reached the door of Thildin's chamber. Utahr rapped three times and paused, then rapped another three times as he was instructed to do. Riedl threw open the door.

"Utahr, we thought you'd never arrive. We've been watching the battle through the window," Riedl said.

"Hurry," Utahr said. "Etain and the baby are safe in the ship, and the king has been taken prisoner. We've got to get out while there's still time. Stay behind me and the men in front. The others will cover us from behind."

Utahr was growing weary, but still he ran on, leading the others to freedom. The hallways were almost quiet now. No sentries came to bar their way. Only the women stood by the doors, talking excitedly but keeping their tones low as the party made their escape.

Finally they entered the passageway from the queen's palace into the gardens. Utahr could see some of the commander's men had gained a position in front of the door. Thildin ran before him, and Riedl ran behind with the commander's men. Only one more row of archers faced the commander's men. Thildin burst outside, and the commander felled an archer who would cut her down with his arrows. Utahr and Riedl ran into the open also. The commander's men ran before them to take them to the safety of the ship.

"Your Majesty, this way!" Utahr said.

Utahr hesitated for a moment to allow Riedl to catch up to him. Again the arrows sang in the air, and Utahr grabbed Riedl and pulled her to the ground.

"Hurry, we're almost there!" He grabbed Riedl's arm and pulled her up. He turned to run again, but an arrow struck him in the breast. The blood of his heart gushed bright red, and he fell with a groan.

Riedl stopped running. "No, no, get up, we're almost there!" she cried. But Utahr did not answer. The arrow had pierced him through the heart, and he was dead. Riedl knealt beside the body, weeping for the one who had loved her since she was a child.

"Oh, no, not you, please, we're going to be free, I promised you would be free," she said.

Thildin looked back when she reached the ship and saw that Utahr had fallen.

"Run, run Riedl, run!" she called out to her; but it was too late. Riedl was already surrounded by the king's sentries. Another line of archers formed against the wall of the queen's palace, and the arrows whirred in the darkness, clattering upon the impenetrable metal of the shuttle.

"Get inside the hatch," Jason said to Thildin.

"But we can't leave her, she'll be executed!" Thildin cried.

"It's too late! I've already lost six men. Come on, get inside the hatch!"

Two of Jason's men took her by the arms and nearly carried her onboard. Weeping, she was brought inside, and the hatch finally closed behind them. Etain and Olara were waiting at the top of the steps to welcome her, as was Gol. As soon as Thildin mounted the steps the three sisters embraced and kissed each other tearfully. Gol stood by and watched them, much moved.

"I never thought this day would come," Olara said.

"I only dreamt it could come true," Etain said, cradling her infant in one arm as she gave Thildin a hug. "But what's the matter? Why are you so upset? Aren't you happy to be out of there?"

"It didn't go as we planned," Thildin said. "One of us was killed, and the princess will surely be executed for treason."

"Do you mean the Princess Riedl?" Etain said.

"Yes," Thildin said. "We couldn't have planned the escape without her. She was my lover and my true friend, and I will never forget her. I can't believe that she must die."

"But we've taken the king prisoner," Olara said. "Perhaps we could bargain for the princess's life."

"I don't know," Thildin said. "Now there will be a coup to put someone else on King Lasher's throne. Whoever comes into power would not want to see the king alive again. If only we could go back and get her! But now we've lost the element of surprise. I don't know how we could ever get in there again."

"Into your seats," Jason said. "It's time to get out of here."

"Yes, sir," Younger said. "Prepare for take-off," he told the pilots at their consoles.

Etain watched as Brown and Johnson dragged the unconscious Lasher unceremoniously and left him in a curious, tall cylinder that gave a three hundred and sixty degree view of its prisoner. He was collared by Younger, and then the door was closed behind him. Etain breathed a sigh of relief and smiled with satisfaction. Only Thildin's grief cast a sharp shadow on her exuberant joy.

Chapter 20

Riedl hung, exhausted, chained to the wall in the Chamber of Virgins. Before her, her half-brother, Ahtaar, paced back and forth with a grin on his face. He can hardly believe he has me here like this, thought Riedl, as she watched her tormentor. She was careful to keep quiet, watching him as he walked back and forth across the floor with unnatural excitement. How quickly he had taken advantage of this emergency to gain power. But Riedl sensed as she observed his slight frame and stooped posture that he in no way had the self-confidence to back his bold move. She was securely bound, but as she watched him the small hope fluttered in her heart that somehow she might gain control.

Ahtaar stopped a moment to stare at his half-sister, shackled so charmingly to the wall. She was very beautiful, he had to admit, with her shiny black curls and svelte body. Her nipples stood out through the coarse muslin gown she had on, and lower down he could also see the silhouette of her puff of black hair. He felt his cock engorge and a tingling in his inner thighs as he looked at her. He wanted badly to prick her, but that would have to be saved for the public deflowering, which would take place before the execution. If he pricked her now, then Gosgovnian law would consider her gotten with child. Then he couldn't execute her; and so his lust would have to wait the three days it would take to try her and kill her.

He had already beaten her with a braided whip. The sensations it gave him flooded him with pleasure. Each time he struck her the whip snapped and forced sudden, muted sounds from her. With each stroke he gave her, he hated her less. He could see the shape of her breasts beneath the coarse dress she wore. He didn't recognize her at all from the time they had played together as children; but as he watched her flinch he saw that she lived up to every one of her legends. He gave her the seven strokes, and then he stopped before her. He had always felt inferior to her, even though it was he who was the natural heir to the throne. A sensation of smallness coursed over him suddenly. It made him avert his eyes from Riedl's face for a moment, and he was very conscious that she had seen it.

Suddenly he needed to pump himself up before her.

"On the day of your execution, before you are beheaded, you will be publicly deflowered by me," said Ahtaar. "Then all the peoples of Gosgovnia, who have heard of your insolence for years, will know how unimportant you really are."

While he was speaking he looked at the floor; but then he looked up to see what effect his words were having on his prisoner. He was met by Riedl's unflinching gaze from coal black eyes. He stopped for a moment, feeling unsure, but then he started again, pacing back and forth across the floor as he continued.

"You consider yourself royalty? For women, the condition doesn't exist," he said. "You are wives or sisters or concubines, to be kept in harems under lock and key, alive only to bear the royal sons and satisfy the cocks of your masters."

He stood in the middle of the floor and looked upon her, but it took all his concentration to meet her gaze steadily.

"And so I will fuck you, and then you will die," he said, beginning his excited walking once more.

Riedl looked on quietly for a moment. She let him know with her eyes that she was watching his nervous pacing.

"And the whipping," she said, "did you enjoy it? I have given many whippings. I enjoy it."

Ahtaar was stunned by the impertinence of her reply. He picked up the braided whip that lay on the floor.

"You need a few more lashes to keep you quiet," he said, and he gave her another seven strokes with the knotted tails.

Riedl tried to shield her face from the strokes with her arms. Each time he struck her, the knots stung on her skin. Though Riedl shrank from the lashing as best she could, Ahtaar had already drawn blood. After the lashes had been given, Riedl hung by her wrists until her small, animal cries had subsided. For a moment she closed her eyes, trying to regain control. When she opened them, she saw Ahtaar had stopped pacing. She could see that he was trying to keep his gaze direct, but frequently his eyes could not meet hers. She concentrated and pictured herself giving him a flogging with the braided whip, and she knew with certainty that if he were her slave he would submit and enjoy it. She felt herself refreshed by this thought and her concentration grew stronger. She allowed powerful images of herself to flow through her mind, images of all the harem girls she had topped, be they willing or cowed. She began to feel sure of herself with Ahtaar. She could win this game. She had played it many times before.

Ahtaar was not looking at her at all now. Still he walked nervously, his arms folded in front of him. Riedl could see he needed to concentrate just to face her. Finally he looked up and steadied himself with another threat.

"Just three more days," he said. "It will be my big day."

Riedl looked at him coolly.

"Why wait?" she said. "Your cock is hard now. I can see it through your trousers. You could take me now, and no one would ever know the difference."

She curled her lips into a pouting smile. She swiveled her body and pushed out her breasts to expose the dark pink nipples that stood out against the fabric of her gown. She felt she was ensnaring him, and the tender folds of her sex began to moisten with the glimmer of pleasure. Ahtaar picked up the braided whip as she knew he would, but this time she played to every stroke. He must see the pleasure of pain, she thought, as the lashes stung upon her skin. The imagery of it must be burned into his untried heart.

"You insolent bitch," he said, but Riedl could see the shiny sweat on his brow.

Ahtaar felt the whip strike every time he hit Riedl as if the blows were falling upon his own skin.

"You insolent bitch!" he said, but each time he struck her he began to fall deeper and deeper under her spell. She was beautiful and fiery and strong. How much he longed for her to mount him and shove her musky cunt onto his rigid cock! He pictured her standing over him as he lay on the ground, her legs parted, spreading the pink folds of her sex with her fingers. He would beg her to throw off her dress of burlap so he could see her goddess's body bathed in the candlelight. Then she would fuck him, and he would know ecstasy.

He found himself standing with the whip in his hand, hungering for her.

"You don't want to leave me now, you love the whip," said Riedl. "You're king now. No one can stop you from satisfying your desires."

He should have raised the whip, but he found its taste didn't suit him. He wanted to untie the princess, this goddess who would surely make him a slave, but every design of his manhood screamed out against it. How much he wanted to kneel before her while she took the head of his prick deep, holding the lips of her sex open to reveal the hungry mouth inside. He must have her, he was king. He dropped the whip, and found himself taking the first step toward her. He was king, he was in control. He would only allow himself a short fucking with her. His manhood would save him from her wiles.

"I do want to fuck you," he said.

"Then untie me," said Riedl.

Ahtaar had already abandoned caution. They were all alone, no one would ever know, and he was king. He went to the wall and cut the leather bracelets with his knife; but instead of sinking to the floor, Riedl stood up straight and proud.

She was taller than he was. She looked at him with her large, shining eyes, and he felt as if his knees were wobbling. His cock was rigid and he felt a melting in his thighs. Suddenly he was anxious about the outline of his cock through his trousers. Was it long enough? Was the head large and dull enough? Anxiety took hold. He was nothing without the whip, nothing, and now she was standing before him, full of beauty, intelligence, and power.

"Are you ready for the princess, Ahtaar? Is this what you had in mind?" said Riedl.

He stood motionless, mesmerized by her pale face and black eyes. He watched her as she moved around him, her eyes never leaving his face. Slowly she reached down to the floor and picked up the whip.

"The lashes can't mark the skin," said Riedl. "Give me your knife."

Ahtaar found himself handing her his knife as she had commanded. He watched her as she cut the knots off the ends of the thongs. Riedl tapped the whip against her thigh.

"How would you like me," she said. "Would you like me to spread my legs and shove my wet sex over your cock?"

Ahtaar winced as she said this and lowered his eyes to the floor.

"Kneel," said Riedl.

Ahtaar was trembling as he sank to the ground. Riedl tapped the whip on her thigh.

"On your knees," she said. "Come here."

Ahtaar slid across the polished wooden floor, shuffling forward on his knees. The floor was hard, and it hurt.

"Hands out in front of you, and keep them there," said Riedl.

Ahtaar found himself obeying her every command.

Riedl walked forward with the whip. She could barely contain her excitement. She lifted the whip up over her head and watched as Ahtaar shuddered. Look at him, she thought, as submissive as a dog. How lucky for her. A smile came to her as she looked at him, his eyes averted, his breaths coming rapidly. She walked to his side and trailed the thongs of the whip across his forehead. Then she walked behind, the whip raised over her head.

"Take off your shirt," she said. "There must be no evidence of the beating."

Ahtaar obeyed, and she was pleased to see how compliant he had become. Now she gave the first stroke of the whip. He cried out in surprise when the stinging lashes struck him.

"Quiet, you dog," she said.

She hit him again, three times in quick succession. This time he only grunted.

"Take off your trousers," she said.

He removed them, lifting his knees enough only to pull them off his legs. Now he was nude before her, kneeling. She struck him on the flank, so that the ends of the thongs stung him on the cock. Then she flogged him on the buttocks, one, two, three.

"Down, you dog, on all fours," she said.

Ahtaar did as she bid him and she went to work on him, slapping and snapping with the long, braided whip. She watched his prick draw into his belly over and over as the biting lashes hit it. She felt her own sex ache and grow plump as she felt the strokes thudding against his back.

Then she paid special attention to his buttocks. His testicles hung down nicely between them. Each time she strapped him she whipped the testicles and the buttocks together. She raised fine red welts on the buttocks, and the testicles grew bright pink and began to swell. She stopped for a moment to admire her handiwork, and then she pressed on.

"You worthless dog," she said, "stay on your knees and expose your prick!"

Ahtaar came back up to a kneeling position, making his belly and penis vulnerable to the whip.

"Arms back, body forward!" said Riedl.

Ahtaar arched his back and thrust his pelvis forward. Then Riedl began to whip him again, this time giving Ahtaar's stiff prick the full force of the lashes. At first his sharp cries intensified, but soon he was grunting deeply. Then his grunts became moans and suddenly he pitched forward and came, his penis spurting short streams of musky semen upon his belly. Afterwards he bent forward, crouching in supplication to the magnificent princess.

Riedl looked down on him, tapping the whip against her thigh. She had made him her slave, but could she get him to come back for more, and so buy herself time? She did not allow herself the luxury of uncertainty. She stepped toward him and spoke boldly.

"This pain will linger," she said, "and tomorrow when you come to me again, you will know even greater pleasure."

As soon as she had spoken, she knew he couldn't resist her.

"You will come tomorrow, as soon as the sun has set," she said. "I will be waiting for you."

She watched as he held his face in his hands, as though weeping.

"You are a queen," he said, and his body shook as he sobbed. Now Riedl could be sure. Yes, the first battle had been won. She looked at her half-brother and her lips curled into a crooked smile. He was born to be a slave. Surely the Goddess was smiling upon her. She raised the whip and ran its thongs across Ahtaar's back once more.

"Get up, dog," she said.

She watched as Ahtaar rose, trembling, from the floor.

"You will be silent in my presence," she said to him, "unless I give you leave to speak. And you will tell no one about today, or you will be ridiculed and forced from the throne for being the born slave that you are."

She began to walk around him in a circle, and she tapped the whip against her thigh to give her words emphasis.

"Now," she said, "you are dismissed. Dress yourself and go."

Silently Ahtaar did as he was bid, and he kept his eyes averted from her at all times while he was preparing to leave. Finally, at the doorway, he looked up at her, and his eyes told Riedl that he was totally hers. She had bought herself time. Perhaps she had even gotten herself the full five days allotted in Gosgovnia for the trial and execution of traitors. He will not be so eager to see me die now, she thought, as she watched him close the door behind him, and she was left alone in the glow of the candlelight once more.

Chapter 21

In the Chamber of the Virgins, Riedl watched through the high crescent window as the last rays of the sun left the sky. As the light faded, the shadows stretched and darkened upon the walls and floor. Soon it would be completely dark and Riedl would be there alone, waiting for Prince Ahtaar to bring the candles. The whip was still on the floor, coiled in the corner. She felt some anxiety while she waited, but she was quick to quell all feelings of doubt. She could not afford to be vulnerable for a moment. She walked over to the corner of the room and picked up the whip. She would have it in her hand when he walked in the door and be fully prepared to make him crawl.

The last glow of daylight still shone in the room. Riedl ran her hand along the length of the whip, fingering its pliant laces as she thought of other ways to master her new slave. She had never played with a man before, and besides, she didn't have her other tools. She rubbed the long black handle of the whip with her fingers. Perhaps it could take the place of a fine ebony cock, she thought to herself. She would have to wet it with her own sex juices, but it could open up a whole new vista of possibilities for subduing the soul of her slave.

She took a few steps across the floor, the rough tiling cool against her bare feet. She trailed the whip behind her and looked over her shoulder at the thirteen laces at the end.

She walked back again to the center of the room, standing before the door. She wanted to be fully prepared when Ahtaar came through the door. She wanted his first glimpse of her to impress him with the image of the magnificent queen.

As she waited she thought of Thildin and Etain. They must have reached Klaerthelke safely by now, and surely they were thinking of her, and how much peril she must be facing. Would they be planning to come back, to make an attempt to rescue her? She only hoped the aliens would listen to Thildin's pleas and return. Every day that she could buy for herself, she knew, would make it more likely that any plan they had for her could succeed.

Fingering the handle of the whip, her attentions returned once more to the situation she faced today. If I could vary our play, she thought, I would have a better chance of holding him for the full five days. Beyond that, no one can save me! She knew the Gosgovnian lords and noblemen would insist on her execution, if only to eliminate yet another royal troublemaker. In recent years King Lasher had conceded more and more to them, to keep them quiet and strengthen his military arm, which owed all its force to the king's vassals. They will be hounding Ahtaar to do away with me, she thought, to impress upon the populace that no one survives the verdict of traitor.

But the five days would be left up to Ahtaar. So soon after the fray, no one dared to usurp his claim to the throne, but Riedl was certain that ultimately there would be a major struggle to name another king. She thought of her half-brother, so slight and unimposing. She wagered few would back him, except for those who believed they would ultimately control him.

Yes, control him, she thought. If only these males knew the secrets of his psyche. She would control him, body and soul, and bring herself to safety and freedom by doing so.

Still the fading sunlight lingered in the room. He would not dare to be tardy, she thought, and angrily she swung the whip with her arm. If he is not here before dark, I will make him pay, she thought. The smallest infraction will bring him the severest punishment. He will revere the dark goddess queen I embody and beg for her fierce attentions. And She will meet out the punishment to the insubordinate male. She will prevail in the end, the Dark Goddess of the harvest that calls all living things back to Her womb.

Finally she heard it, the doorknob turning in the door. Slowly the door creaked open, as Ahtaar made his way timidly into the room. He carried a bag of black leather with him, and Riedl presumed this was for the candles. Riedl spread her feet out on the floor, and began to tap with the whip against her thigh. The game had begun.

He came in and closed the door, his eyes averted to the floor.

"Dog," said Riedl. "Do you know how close you were to being late? It's almost dark. Where are the candles? Would you leave the Goddess without light? I will whip you hard for this."

Ahtaar reached into his bag and drew out the tallow candles. Silently he worked, putting the tapers carefully into the sconces upon the wall.

"Kneel," said Riedl.

Immediately Ahtaar kneeled, obeying the princess, his head bowed and his arms folded in supplication. Riedl could see that he already had a hard erection.

"Body forward, dog," she said. "Taste the whip for your insolence."

She flogged him with the lashes, paying special attention to his hard penis, raising faint whelps with the leather traces. Ahtaar was so much under her spell he began to moan instantly.

Riedl whipped him solidly. He moaned and moaned as the leather traces stung his cock, leaving it hard, pink, and swollen.

"Expose the head of your prick," said Riedl. "It must be whipped, since it will never push and prod the wet sex of the goddess queen. Push it forward with your fist. I've been reserving a special whipping for it, to make you come like a dog at Her feet."

With a groan Ahtaar took his penis in his hand, and pushed it forward so its head would take the blows of the whip. He groaned again as the lashes of the whip stung the small mouth of his prick, and he kept on groaning, writhing in place, as Riedl plied the whip to the head of the prick expertly. Soon the small mouth of Ahtaar's penis had bright pink lips that pouted out, and then his cries came in quick succession. Then he came, spurting streams of semen that burned the red hole at the very tip of his penis. Only then did the whipping stop, and Riedl laughed, holding the whip by her side, prodding Ahtaar's scrotum with the ends of her toes and thrusting out her breasts against the poor muslin dress that she wore.

"Dog," she said, "you will come again tonight, at the feet of the Great One, for She commands it, and your male seed shall spill again on the floor of this prison. You will know Her again, wholly, and you will be penetrated like a woman; and then you will come and come like the dog you are, and through you all the males of your race will know the true place of their souls."

Then Riedl moved forward, spreading the lips of her sex.

"Lick, you dog," she said. "Lick the Gate of Life, as you have never done with your concubines. Lick the Gate of Life. For it will swallow you once more, all of you."

Then she thrust her pelvis forward, back and forth, savoring the strokes of his obedient tongue.

"Harder, dog, harder!" she cried, as the lapping of his tongue fell upon the folds of her cunt. But he failed to rub the pleasure bud, which was engorged, and briskly she meted out punishment with the whip, raising the limp penis to a state of inflammation once more.

She bent her knees and thrust her pelvis even further forward, splaying the crevice with her fingers.

"Lick," she cried, and "lick," once more; but her slave continued to grovel, and only licked her sex with the timid licks of the slave awaiting punishment. She whipped him as he stood on all fours, making sure the head of his penis received the lashing it deserved. Then she took a step backward, and began prodding her cunt with the handle of the whip, wetting the end with the rich juices of her sex.

"Buttocks forward," she said. Ahtaar hesitated for just a moment, until he realized that she wanted his buttocks facing her. Then he turned himself, positioning his testicles and buttocks for a wanton lashing.

But Riedl surprised him. She gave him just a few strokes with the whip, and then she stepped forward and commanded him to spread the cheeks of his buttocks with his hands. Still leaning forward, he did as the Queen Goddess commanded him.

"Your hole," said Riedl, "Expose your hole."

Ahtaar nearly touched his chin to the floor as he spread the cheeks of his buttocks with his hands.

Then Riedl took the handle of the whip, which she had moistened with the juices of her cunt, and she began to press on Ahtaar's brown hole, circling and pressing, until she heard Ahtaar moan out loud. She circled and pressed, circled and pressed, until Ahtaar's brown hole began to open and give way.

"Spread, you dog," she cried, and soon she was working the handle of the whip just inside the brown hole of Ahtaar, in a little, out a little, while Ahtaar's moans intensified, deepening into grunts and groans of pleasure. Then, with a single thrust, Riedl sank the handle of the whip deep inside Ahtaar's exposed hole, and then she worked it, up and down, up and down, and all the while Ahtaar's grunts came deeper and faster, until finally Riedl made a very deep thrust and he came again, spurting his grayish come upon the wooden floor before Riedl's feet.

Immediately Riedl gave his buttocks three more lashes with the whip, and then she stood with her legs spread, laughing at him.

"Your brown hole aches for the Goddess, doesn't it?" she said. "Your hole aches to receive the Goddess, as few males will ever know Her. Lap up your semen from the floor!"

Ahtaar began to lick his come off the floor, and Riedl continued to admonish him.

"Tomorrow you will receive the Goddess into your body once more, and your penis will feel the whip. Think on it, while you wait to return to me," said Riedl.

At that Ahtaar stopped licking and looked up from the floor, but remained mute, as she had commanded. Riedl stepped forward so she could give him another few strokes with the whip.

"Tomorrow you will return before the light has faded from this room, and with you, you shall bring the leather wallet filled with the things I specify," said Riedl. "First, you will bring a pair of leather bracelets, so I can bind you to the wall, like the dog you are."

Riedl began to circle him, tapping her thigh with the whip.

"Next, you will bring three polished cocks of various sizes, so I can penetrate you more easily than I can with the whip handle. I enjoy it more then," she said.

"You will also bring a falconer's jess, swivel, and leash," she said. "I have some new games in mind for you when you return."

She moved in front of him and stood there, her stance bold beneath her undyed dress.

"That is all," she said. "Go."

Ahtaar rose slowly then, and Riedl watched him in silence, thinking about what the days ahead of her would bring, until finally he carefully closed the chamber door behind him and was gone.

Chapter 22

"Shh, Brida, shh," said Etain.

She cradled her new infant in her arms and prepared to give her the breast. Before her King Lasher was bound and collared in the tube. It was a remarkable device, really, thought Etain, as the baby nursed quietly. Some force that emanated from the tube bound Lasher's wrists. Etain didn't understand it, but she had watched Jason's crewmembers perform operations on the console of the bridge, and they could release or bind Lasher's wrists by clicking with a rolling device on great screens that lay before them on the console. The aliens' ship with its artificial environment was impressive enough, but she marveled at the tube, a device that kept a man prisoner, yet kept him cool and dry as well. Besides, there was no chance of escape. The clear material it was made of was unbreakable, and it opened only by operation of the computer console on the bridge. She had seen it used when Lasher was first put inside. The console emitted a tone, and then a red light blinked from a point at the top of the tube. The crewmember that had been assigned the responsibility of the care of the prisoner could lower in meals by means of the console, and then he could release Lasher's wrists so he could feed himself, all without opening the tube.

Etain thought that after Sillessa Brida had finished nursing, she would hold her up for Lasher to see. He stood in front of her with his wrists bound before him, looking, she thought, rather sullen. She remembered how many times she had stood like that before him, and every humiliation he had ever given her, and now the sight of him made her glad; yet she did not smile or jeer at him, for she had some affection for him still. She just looked on solemnly, without showing her true feelings. Finally she spoke to him, for as she watched him in his degraded condition in the tube, she knew he was becoming angrier and angrier.

"So much has happened," she said, carefully watching Lasher's expression, "but perhaps we can all become friends again someday. You can stay here with us, and you will be well treated, except, of course, you will have to wear a collar. Other than that, there will be nothing to make you feel like a prisoner. Once we have your assurance that you will be well-behaved, we can let you out of the tube."

Lasher struggled against the binding force that held his wrists and replied angrily.

"Never," he said. "The Gosgovnian army will over run this place, and I will be set free. Then all of you will pay the price for humiliating the leader of the greatest empire Gwaehr has ever known."

Etain looked at him calmly.

"I think not," she said, "for there are many in the royal court of Gosgovnia who would conspire to take your place on the throne. You did not always rule justly, Lasher, and now the time has come for you to pay the price."

As Etain said this, she thought of Kodohr, who must be caught up in the fray at the royal palace since the king had been abducted. Would she ever see him again? Would he come to seek her out in this far off land? For a moment her heart was filled with sadness, but quickly she turned her thoughts to happier matters, grateful that she and her baby were alive, safe, and free.

Lasher did not answer her, but only struggled against his invisible restraints, pulling with his fingers at the hated collar he wore around his neck. Etain could see that he was far too angry to be reasoned with. She thought of asking Commander Jason if he could release Lasher from his wrist restraints at least, but then decided against it, thinking that Lasher might throw himself against the walls of the tube and cause a ruckus. Besides, she thought to herself, Lasher must first learn to take the punishments he has so frequently meted out to others before he should be rewarded with more lenient treatment. She decided to leave Lasher until he cooled down and see to the welfare of her sister, Thildin, instead. She knew Thildin was suffering sorely, in constant anxiety over the fate of her companion, Riedl. Again she thought of Kodohr. How ironic it is, thought Etain, that now that we are finally free, we should be missing what life brought us in our days of captivity.

Sillessa Brida had finished nursing. Etain moved her so the baby was cradled against her shoulder, and then she left the bridge and walked down the cool white corridor to Thildin's quarters. There she stopped in front of the sliding metal door, with its softly glowing aquamarine finish, and touched the lit panel with her fingers for permission to enter. A low tone sounded and the door slid open, and Etain saw Thildin coming to greet her.

"Hello," said Thildin. "I'm so glad to see you. How's the baby?"

"She's fine," said Etain. "I just wanted to see how you're doing. This waiting must be hard."

"It is, very much," said Thildin. "I know Commander Jason needs time to prepare for another foray back to Gosgovnia, but if he doesn't hurry, Riedl will surely be dead before we can have a chance to save her. And I have so much guilt! How could I have left her behind like that?"

Thildin lowered her eyes to the floor, and Etain could see that Thildin was struggling not to cry.

"You can't think like that," said Etain, "you know you mustn't. What choice did you have? Waiting for her would have put us all into jeopardy. And have hope! The commander has agreed to go back for her. We have some time. You know that even in Gosgovnia it requires some process to deal with a traitor, especially if that person is the daughter of the king. We have only been back two days. Commander Jason has promised that he will be ready in the next day or two."

"But you know that might be too late," said Thildin.

"I know it sounds like it will take forever," said Etain, "but we've cast our spell for victory, and now there is nothing to do but wait. I hate to see you going through this. There isn't a one of us here who wouldn't do almost anything to spare you of it."

"I know," said Thildin, "Thank you. I don't want to sound ungrateful."

"Never," said Etain.

"And what about Olara and Gol, have they arrived yet?"

"They hadn't when I left the bridge."

Thildin curled her lips into a wry smile.

"And how is King Lasher doing?" she said.

"I suppose as well as can be expected," said Etain. "You should see him, cornered there in that tube. Come out of your room, come out for a walk with me. It will do you good. We can go back to the bridge and meet

Olara and Gol there when they get here. We might even take a walk outside. We're free now, and it's a beautiful day."

"All right," said Thildin.

She reached with her foot under the bed and slipped into her sandals.

"I'm ready to go," said Thildin. "Here, let me take Brida."

Etain handed the baby to Thildin, and they walked over to the heavy aquamarine door. Thildin fingered the lit panel and the door slid open for them.

They stepped into the narrow white hallway, which was crowded with the business of the Nu Omega 7 Operation this weekday at noon. Etain and Thildin walked past dozens of humanoid crewmembers who were on the job, and the computer diodes blinked silently in the consoles that lined the hallway's curvilinear border. The window shields had been opened, and so bright rays of sunlight streamed in, augmenting the artificial lighting of the ship most pleasantly. Thildin began to feel her mood improving.

As they neared the bridge, Etain said, "Please don't tease Lasher when you see him, for my sake. He's the father of my child. I'm hoping that maybe, with time, he can come to accept his fate, just as at his hands we had to accept ours. It would be a lot easier. And we can never send him back, since as long as he is here we are almost guaranteed the Gosgovnians will not invade."

"Yes, he was hated," said Thildin. "But it will be hard for me to hide my true feelings for him. I promise to try, though, for your sake, as you ask."

They came to the bridge, where they saw that Olara and Gol had arrived. Commander Jason was also there, and the three of them were engaged in conversation. Immediately Thildin saw Lasher, imprisoned in the tube, but she decided to say nothing to him.

"Hello," said Olara. She went to Thildin and embraced her and the baby. "I'm so glad to see you, you look much better. We were just talking to Commander Jason about his plan to return to Gosgovnia."

Lasher stirred in his tube, trying to free his hands, but only Thildin looked up at him, and she decided to ignore him.

"Yes," said Jason, "It looks like we can be ready by tomorrow night." To Thildin he said, "I'll need you to come with us, of course. I know you must know the palaces well."

"That's not completely true," said Thildin. "At least, for me it isn't. We weren't allowed access to the whole palace, only to a few rooms and corridors."

"But I can never forget the way to the Chamber of Virgins," said Etain. "Surely that is where they are keeping Princess Riedl. All virgins of noble birth are kept there to await their fate. I'm certain we'll find her there."

She turned to Lasher.

"Don't you think that's true?" said Etain.

Lasher only grunted in anger.

"Can you find your way there from the outside?" said Jason.

"Yes, of course," said Etain. "All you have to do is get into the northwest passage way, just inside the northern wall of the palace gardens. Then you just go down the first hallway. The Chamber of Virgins will be behind the first door that you see."

"Excellent," said Jason. "You and Thildin will remain aboard, of course, while a squadron of men and I go down to do the actual rescue. You should be safe that way. How does that sound? Can you handle it?"

"Yes, that sounds very good," said Thildin, while Etain nodded. "And you think you will be ready to go tomorrow night?"

"Yes, I'm sure of it," said Jason.

"That's wonderful. I think we can still make it to her in time," said Thildin, and with that she smiled and held baby Sillessa Brida out for Olara to hold. "Here, take her," said Thildin. "Look at her, she's so beautiful."

"Sure, give her to me," said Olara. "It's good to see a smile on your face. I think we can do it, don't you?"

"Yes," said Thildin. "I think we'll be able to rescue her. But I wish we were at home, so we could make a sacrifice in the temple. Commander Jason, perhaps we could trouble you for some more candles. We don't have an altar, but we can put them up in the windowsill of my room."

"Wait, I'll help you," said Olara. "Here, Gol, take Brida. Maybe you two could wait for us, and then we could all take a walk outside," she said to Gol and Etain.

"And I'll send the steward with the candles to your room," said Jason.

"Thank you," said Thildin. "We'll be waiting for them. Come on," she said to Olara, "let's go."

"We'll see you later," said Olara, and with that the two women left the bridge, heading down the ship's narrow corridor to make their candle magic.

Chapter 23

On the eve of her third night in captivity, Riedl waited in the Chamber of Virgins while the sunlight faded from the pink and gold sky. The first date of her execution had passed. She should have been taken that morning to the platform in the square of Gelstohr, there to have the hideous sentence of the Gosgovnian court passed upon her. Instead, she had escaped another day, all because of her seduction of the slave-prince Ahtaar. Now yet again she awaited his arrival, and she stood excitedly brandishing the whip, knowing the door to the chamber would open very soon.

She had thought of a new scheme to occupy Ahtaar's tastes when he arrived. But first he will have the ritual whipping as always, she thought. Time enough to add more inventive play as the night wears on.

She thought of Thildin and the alien ship. Surely Thildin will have convinced them to come back and get me, she thought. But when will they arrive, tonight? But what if they should fail? Will Thildin know where to find me? A pulse of anxiety thrilled through her, but immediately she calmed herself, careful not to be vulnerable for a moment.

The shadows grew tall on the far wall of the chamber. The tall wardrobe threw a shadow of its own, jutting out across the floor and extending almost to the doorway of the chamber. Riedl followed the pattern of the barred window with her eyes as it stretched out upon the floor, her thoughts racing as she waited for Ahtaar. She wondered if she would hear the alien ship coming, or perhaps after it landed, so that she might be ready for them when they burst through the door, and she could handle Ahtaar so he could not interfere with their plans. She began to fantasize that they would come that night. How wonderful it would be to be released from this prison and saved! In excitement she flicked the handle of the whip, striking the bars of the shadows that were projected onto the floor. The Goddess is with me, she thought, we will succeed! Now she stood with great hope in her heart, waiting for the door to open.

Then she heard the creak of the door on its hinges, and she turned so she would be facing Ahtaar when he entered the room. She could see he was trembling as he looked into her eyes, and then he lowered his eyes to the ground. From his shoulder hung the black leather wallet, which Riedl had instructed him to bring.

"Down, slave," she said, "and give me the bag. I have new plans for you tonight, after you get your whipping. Undress yourself."

Ahtaar handed Riedl the bag, fingers trembling. Then he got down on his knees and started to disrobe. Riedl could see he was already beginning to sweat. She slung the bag over her shoulder and reached in with her hand. Inside the bag she found the candles, which she put into the sconces on the walls. After she had lit them she rummaged in the bag and found what she wanted, the falconer's jess, swivel, and leash. She also found the polished cocks she had ordered him to bring, but these did not interest her for the moment. Ahtaar just kneeled on the floor naked, his head bowed, waiting. At the sight of him Riedl smiled. His penis was still soft and limp, but it had just begun to elongate as the first waves of pleasure stirred through him.

"Come forward," said Riedl.

Ahtaar moved across the floor on his knees. When he was kneeling directly in front of her, eyes still averted to the floor, Riedl said, "On your hands and knees."

Ahtaar got down on all fours. Riedl felt her sex begin to thicken and moisten with pleasure.

"Turn yourself," she said. "I want your buttocks first."

Ahtaar did as he was told. As he turned around, Riedl could see that his cock was beginning to grow hard as he anticipated the first lashes of the whip. She raised the whip high, preparing to give the first stroke. Then she began to whip him, and as each stroke fell upon his naked skin, she felt her cunt grow wetter and hotter.

She whipped him well, forcing a deep grunt from him with each blow. She made sure to strike his testicles from time to time, even though they drew up to his body, until she was satisfied that they were sufficiently reddened and hot. Then she walked around Ahtaar till she was facing him sideways, and she gave his left flank a vigorous lashing, making sure that his hard cock was stung by the whip's laces.

Ahtaar's grunts were coming shorter and harder now, and Riedl could see that he was panting and sweating as he came closer and closer to climax. When she saw that he was nearly ready to come, she stopped the whipping abruptly.

"You won't get your pleasure so easily today," she said. "I have a new trial for you to endure."

She reached into the black leather bag and pulled out the falconer's jess, swivel, and leash.

"Straighten your knees, and spread eagle," she said.

Ahtaar kept his hands on the floor and straightened his legs, so that his buttocks were high in the air. Then he spread his feet apart on the floor, so that his testicles dangled unfettered. His hard prick was drawn up tight against his belly.

Riedl took the jess and swivel and reached under Ahtaar's belly, grasping his hard penis in her hand. She slipped the jess over the head of his cock, and pulled the trace taut till the jess was seated tightly and painfully around the neck of Ahtaar's penis. Then she attached the swivel and leash, so that she could pull on the tightly fastened jess as she desired. With the first tug she gave the leash Ahtaar moaned deeply. Riedl was well satisfied with the potential of her device. She pulled and pulled sharply, making the tight jess bite into the flesh of Ahtaar's penis, and as she did Ahtaar's cries and gasps began to come high pitched and quickly. His legs began to wobble, but she gave him a hard thrust against his testicles with the handle of the whip.

"Up," she said, "get your ballocks up. Spread your legs, dog. I'm not finished with you yet."

She reached into the black bag and pulled out a glossy black cock of polished ebony. She passed it between her own legs to moisten it with the juices of her sex, and then she plunged it into Ahtaar's brown hole. Now she pulled steadily on the jess, while she worked Ahtaar's nether hole with the cock. Finally Ahtaar gave a loud grunt and he came, spurting his pearly semen on the floor. He collapsed on the floor into his own come, still moaning with pleasure. Riedl dropped the leash and stepped over his prone figure, facing him from the other side.

"Lay there as you are," she said. "Wallow in your own liquids.

Remove the jess from your cock, and clean it with your tongue."

Riedl could see that Ahtaar was spent, but she was not through with him yet. I must keep him occupied, she thought, for what if they might be coming for me tonight? Again she felt a twinge of doubt, but she did not show her true feelings, and broadened her stance instead. She dropped the ebony cock and rapped with the whip on her thigh. She raised the whip and gave him a blow.

"Lick, dog," she said, "and when you have finished with the jess, you will clean the cock as well."

Ahtaar, exhausted, began to sob brokenly, but he did as he was told, licking his come off the leather jess. Riedl couldn't have been more satisfied with the results of their session. Now, she thought, now, if only they would arrive, while I have him so entirely overcome by my spell. Silently she prayed to the Goddess for her rescue. Ahtaar had finished cleaning the jess, and she kicked the ebony cock over to him for him to clean as well. He was still uttering small, gasping sobs, but diligently he took the cock and began to lap it clean.

Then, as she stood over Ahtaar, tapping with the whip against her thigh, she heard a muted, rattling sound. She held her breath while Ahtaar kept on with his task, hoping to hear something, anything again. There it was again, a clattering noise, louder now, as if it were drawing nearer, and then again, louder still, and hope sprang up in Riedl's heart, while the miserable slave kept on with his task, unaware of anything except the majesty of her presence.

Again, louder. Now it was as if she heard footsteps coming, and voices calling out in excitement, although she could not make out the words. Ahtaar heard too, and he dropped the ebony cock and raised his torso from the floor, turning his head to look behind him at the chamber door. Riedl saw his mouth drop open, and quickly she put her foot down hard upon his back and gave him another stroke with the whip, but he was rallying and she was afraid she would not be able to keep him down.

"Down, slave," she said, and she whipped him again, kicking him in the throat to master him, anything now to remain in control. He gasped for breath and writhed on the floor, but she kicked him again and then put her foot upon his back once more, whipping and whipping, keeping him down, buying the precious minutes that could mean she would live and be free.

Then suddenly the door burst open, and in rushed a squadron of soldiers, dressed in black and armed with their small, shiny weapons. Ahtaar tried to rise, but it was too late. The leader of the squadron pointed his weapon at him, and he fell motionless to the floor.

"Come on," he shouted out to Riedl, waving with his arm. She could not understand his language, but his meaning was clear enough. She ran into the corridor with soldiers before and behind her, and then they were in the passageway, heading for the doorway to the garden.

"Get down," the commander said, and a Gosgovnian arrow whizzed past them, until the commander's pistol felled the archer with a flash. And then Riedl was running again, out into the open garden, not daring to look behind her as she ran for the alien ship, thinking only of Thildin and freedom, hoping against hope that her life might be spared.

An archer stepped in front of her and drew on his bow. Riedl screamed and dropped to the ground, afraid that she would meet the same fate as the dear and true friend, Utahr. One of the aliens caught the Gosgovnian in the light of his pistol and saved her.

"Run, run!" he said, and Riedl was on her feet once more, panting for air and stumbling forward, running for her life.

And then it was if she entered a dream. She didn't feel herself moving, but she saw the ship grow closer and closer. She fought for air and her legs grew leaden, but somehow she kept her feet moving, up and down, up and down. She could almost make out the faces of the soldiers who were guarding the ship's hatch. Just a little farther, just a little bit more, she thought, and suddenly she burst through the circle of guards with the soldiers close behind her, and strong hands took her by the arms and led her up the steps into the ship.

And there, at the top of the stairs, were Thildin and Etain. Riedl heard the hatch of the ship closing as she rushed into Thildin's arms, tears of gladness spilling on her cheeks. Riedl tried to speak, but she was so breathless she found she could not.

"I can hardly believe it's true," said Thildin, and Riedl saw that Thildin, too, was overcome with tears.

"Prepare to take off," said the commander. "Take your seats," he said to Thildin and Etain in E'Hrglaendi.

Hurriedly Thildin led Riedl to their seats, and made sure that they were both securely strapped in. Etain was already in her seat, ready for the ship's take-off.

"Seven, six, five, four, three, two, one, blast off," said the commander, and immediately Riedl heard the ship's engines firing as the shuttle rose straight into the air. She took Thildin's hand, and noticed she was trembling. She was finally catching her breath, and it felt as though her limbs were melting into her seat; but none of that made any difference, she could afford to be vulnerable now. The Goddess had answered her petitions. Thankfully she offered a prayer of reverence, for the impossible had come to pass. She was still alive, and she was free.

Chapter 24

"Younger, get your ass over here," said Jason, as he stood before the window on the bridge.

Younger grinned and walked over to the window.

"Yes, sir," he said, as he stood at Jason's side.

"Just look at that view," said Jason. "Damn beautiful, isn't it?"

Together they looked out onto a world filled with sunlight, the long green grass and wild shaerl lilies moving gracefully in the breeze. Everything in the green valley still glowed with life as the long warm days began to pass, and Indian summer approached on the thorny, leggy stems of golden mildin flowers.

"Yes, sir, said Younger. "It sure is beautiful. Good to be back, isn't it?"

Jason looked up at him, but Younger could see that he was preoccupied with some thought. He was frowning, and his black eyes seemed wider and more serious than usual. Younger thought of asking him what he had on his mind, but decided that he might be intruding, and so he hesitated. After a moment Jason looked away, and began gazing out of the window again.

"What do you want to do," said Jason, "after we leave Gwaehr?"

"What do you mean, sir?" asked Younger.

"Oh, stop with the 'sir.' I mean, what do you want to do after our operation on this planet is completed? What do you want to do with your life?"

Younger was surprised. In all the time he and Jason had been friends such a serious conversation had never taken place.

"Oh, I don't know," said Younger. "I guess I'll just move on to the next job. Hopefully I'll find some women, wherever I end up."

"Yeah, women," said Jason. "Hey, have you ever been in love?"

Younger looked more closely at the commander. Certainly he was acting very strangely. Could he be ill?

"What did you say?" said Younger.

"You heard me," said Jason, "I said, have you ever been in love."

"Well, I guess I was, once, when I was about sixteen years old. She stiffed me though."

"Don't give me when you were sixteen," said Jason. "I want to know have you ever felt anything, anything at all, for a woman."

"Sure, I've felt for them, but I wouldn't call it love," said Younger. Younger was growing increasingly uncomfortable with the conversation. He was afraid he was going to be asked next if he had ever been in love with a man.

"Say," Younger said, "why don't we go for some coffee?"

"Naw," said Jason, "I think I'll just stay here. You go on. I'll catch up to you later."

Now Younger was really concerned, but he didn't know what to do. This was the first time Jason had missed their morning coffee in five years. He decided to shrug it off, and leave Jason with his thoughts for a while.

"Okay," said Younger. "I'll catch you later."

Jason nodded and didn't look behind him as Younger left him standing at the window. God, thought Jason, as he stared out into the morning, this planet is full of beauty. It'll be hard to leave it, he thought. It'll be hard to leave this place, and it will be hard to leave that woman.

That woman. Now that Younger had left him, he was fully free to occupy himself with visions of Riedl. Her shining eyes, her black curls, the outline of her slender, shapely body beneath that homespun gown. How badly he wanted to caress her, kiss her, finger her cunt until it was wet with the juices of sex. God, he thought, I shall never forget the sight of her standing there with that whip, keeping that weasel under her heel. He felt a pang as he realized that she embodied everything he could want in a woman. She was nothing less than magnificent.

He moved away from the window, brooding, and looked around him on the bridge. There were only three crewmembers there. Everything on the ship was in order, status quo, right as rain, but he felt himself changed. All he could do was think of her. Maybe I need a drink, he thought to himself, but he knew he could never drink away the pull he felt on all his sensibilities.

But Riedl, he knew, had her heart set on other things. Soon she, Thildin, and Etain would be inducted into the Goddess's temple in Klaerthelke, until they could return to the ruined homeland of E'Hrglaend. Then she would be able to follow in the path of the Great Goddess, and that was what she truly wanted, thought Jason. That, and he knew Riedl was already in love with Thildin. What luck, he thought, that I should finally fall for a female, and she should turn out to scorn men.

He thought about all the women he had ever known who had been feminists. None of them had ever been through what Riedl had experienced. The men, of course, sneered and joked about it, about how feminists were all just a bunch of bitches who needed to get laid, but in his heart Jason knew that they were right. Men did subjugate women, in all the known places of the universe, and sometimes in the most hideous ways.

But he would never be able to get all that straight, not in his lifetime. He wondered what it might have been like if he and Riedl had met under different circumstances, if it might have been different if she didn't have every reason to shun men. But I only think that, he told himself, because I would like to believe that it was her destiny to meet me, when, in fact, it was my destiny to meet her.

He sighed. It was a hopeless situation. Did his crew find him a changed man? He looked around him at the familiar bridge and decided that no one would ever know except himself, and perhaps Younger. He thought of Younger and their long companionship, and wondered why men never talked about the importance of friends.

Well, he would join Younger for coffee. He would think about Riedl some other time, lie awake and picture her, dream of holding her hand. So much for the twists of the lives of men. He thought of Riedl's goddess, and found himself praying a small prayer, that She might always make Riedl's burdens few, her steps light, and the days in Her path many, happy, and fruitful.